LETTERS FROM CARTHAGE

Recent Titles by the Author from Severn House

DOUBLE JEOPARDY
FORGET IT
KING'S FRIENDS
THE LAST ENEMY
HEAR ME TALKING TO YOU
TIP TOP

THE SIXTH MAN and other stories

LETTERS FROM CARTHAGE

BILL JAMES

This first world edition published in Great Britain 2007 by
SEVERN HOUSE PUBLISHERS LTD of
9–15 High Street, Sutton, Surrey SM1 1DF.
This first world edition published in the USA 2007 by
SEVERN HOUSE PUBLISHERS INC of
595 Madison Avenue, New York, N.Y. 10022.

British Library Cataloguing in Publication Data

James, Bill, 1929-
    Letters from Carthage
    1.   Suburban life - Fiction
    2.   Detective and mystery stories
    I.   Title
    823.9'14 [F]

    ISBN-13: 978-0-7278-6460-4 (cased)
    ISBN-13: 978-0-7278-9192-1 (paper)

Letters from Carthage is developed from Bill James' short
story *At Home* which appears in the collection *The Sixth Man
and other stories* (Severn House, 2006)

All Severn House titles are printed on acid-free paper.

Typeset by Palimpsest Book Production Ltd.,
Grangemouth, Stirlingshire, Scotland.
Printed and bound in Great Britain by
MPG Books Ltd., Bodmin, Cornwall.

1

*W*e're new here. I suppose you could call us jumped-up. Well, I don't think I mind being jumped-up. What's the alternative? Being stuck? Or worse, going down? Naturally, my husband, Vince, and I have heard all the sneering stuff said about suburbia, or 'the burbs' as they're mockingly called. But if you come from the inner city, like us, the burbs don't seem too bad at all. I'm in favour of a bit of quiet if it means no drive-by fire power from thugs. I'll accept some dullness if dullness means no pimping or grievous bodily harm on the street corner. So far, I don't believe any group of young women celebrating New Year locally has been gun blasted outside a club, as happened in Birmingham not long ago.

There's suburbia and suburbia. This is superior suburbia. I like that. The houses are detached, four- or five-bedroomed properties, good gardens front and back, considerable hedges, double garages, coach lamps alongside sizeable square porches. Next stop, a mansion. The mortgage hurts, but we had a decent deal because of the market slump. Luckily, we'd been renting. Vince said, 'Let's act now and buy the best we can, Kate.' We haven't run into any of the stand-offishness that's supposed to exist in these neighbourhoods. True, people don't blurt out their whole life story immediately, but most seem friendly. We've chatted outside to the couple next door but one, Jill and Dennis Seagrave, though without being asked into their house, Carthage, yet. And a woman further along has offered to brief me on the best shopping hereabouts! We've got the education, Vincent *and I, and enough money to go with it now. We'll fit in all right.*

I've said people in these sorts of areas can be a little reticent, but we did learn from the Seagraves that they've lived in Tabbett Drive for four years and have been married for twelve. They seem happy and settled. Dennis is some sort of broker and into hedge sculpture – topiary; a true skill. He has fashioned a wonderful peacock in the privet of their front garden. You won't see many of those in Peckham. Watching the Seagraves and listening, neither Vince nor I sensed any really troublesome angst *in their relationship, though twelve years is a fair while, no question.*

2

Carthage
Tabbett Drive
Exall DL2 4NG
20 May 2005

My dearest Mother,

I would have replied sooner but . . . well, Dennis is in and out of the house at odd times and I don't feel safe with pen and paper. He notices. It's all right this afternoon. He has definitely gone to town, and I would hear the car early enough to get things out of sight if he came back unexpectedly. Mind you, Mother, I still maintain there's quite a lot to be said in favour of Dennis, regardless.

How lovely it was to hear your voice on the phone a few weeks ago! Nobody speaks my name the way you do. I can hear it now – 'Jill? Jill, that you, darling?' – so gentle and affectionate. But, please, when phoning don't ever say anything,

I mean anything DIFFICULT. Well, I know you won't. You realize the situation. There are three extensions here, making matters a bit dicey, you see, and we are all the time plugged into a hi-tech record-and-answer machine which logs disconnections of any extension, and he would want to know why I'd done it, in that suspicious way of his. So damn crazy, really, isn't it, that all this arm-and-a-leg electronic gear for communication by phone makes it necessary to be in touch by letter – that utterly antique means of keeping contact! I'm sure you know that in times past people used to write stories – I mean whole, very hefty books that were done entirely as letters, like *Clarissa*, about a girl getting seduced, which was on TV. Those days, they really took their time getting raped! Well, I hope nobody ever makes a book out of *our* letters, Mum. Dennis often reads them, in his little, sneaky way.

I just glanced back at what I've written . . . Oh, when I say I don't feel safe, I'm not sure why I said that, and the last thing I want is for you to worry. 'Safe' is such a major word. I don't think he would really go beyond, you know, not in a *major* way. My feeling is that Denn's really yellow deep down. Well, I'm 101 per cent careful all the time not to antagonize. Knowing me, you'd be surprised at your daughter's efforts in the cause of peace! I feel like the Arbitration Service! I do things absolutely as he wants now, more or less, and he can really be quite sunny. Well, obviously. That was the side he always used to show. Mum, I know I could still love him. I know it, know it, if only he would stay like that for a little while, say weeks. I want to, *long* to, love him. But there are these sudden falls into . . . well, shall we call it turbulence?

I mustn't go on worrying you, though. Yes, of course, it would be grand if you came to visit. Don't worry. He would be fine, rest assured. In your letter you said some dates and I've remembered them. I hold important facts like that in my head. Yes, September or October would be wonderful. I don't keep your letters, so this would make it hard for someone to turn them into a book, as mentioned jokingly earlier! It's a precaution, that's all. Another precaution. The first precaution, of course, is that I asked you to send any of your letters meant only for me, and containing personal, private matter, *not* to this address, Carthage, but to my neighbour's house instead. It's wiser. He checks the mail arriving here. Alice, the neighbour, is a real gem. Of course, when you write to me it is 'care of Mrs AV Ward.' I bought her an azalea. I feel I owe her so much gratitude. Alice leaves me alone with your latest letter in her sitting room for as long as I like, and gives me tea and biscuits. It's so pleasant. Sometimes she likes to be called Alice, sometimes Veronica. It depends on how she sees herself that particular day. It's harmless. She's a treasure, though heavyish in the hip region. I'd say she's got her eye on Dennis, the quaint old piece. Yes, women do take to him, Ma, despite everything, even a woman like Mrs AV Ward, who's in line for an OBE, as I hear.

I go over and over your lovely writing, and then down her hall toilet it goes in teeny-weeny little bits. That sounds horrible, I know, but it *is* best, believe me. This amounts to the second precaution. You see, by then I have read the letter so often that I can remember all the sweet, sweet words, and this is enough until the next one arrives and Mrs AV Ward lets me know. This would be via a nod in the Drive or at, say, Tesco's, but not by phone, obviously, because he might be about and earholing, in that chummy little style he has. The flush doesn't always take everything away, and she understands if I repeat. It would be unwise to have something like one of your letters in the house with me here. He looks around quite a bit in his dismal little fashion.

But when you write about coming . . . Mum, sorry, I'll break off now because I hear the car. I'll post this as it is, when I get a chance. Half a letter is better than none!

Please, Mother, do not fret.

Your loving daughter,
Jill

3

What Vince and I really like about the Seagraves is that they don't seem to be just types. Do you know what I mean? All right, as I've said, where we live is your standard bit of high-quality suburbia and people are supposed to fit a profile. Jill and Dennis are not like that. And Vince and I hope we are not like it ourselves, naturally. We're new to the area, anyway, and wouldn't have had time to slip into conformity, even if we wanted to. I feel a little like the I Am A Camera notion, putting an outsider's, so far unaffected eye over things. And what I record – at this stage, anyway – is that the Seagraves are a lovely example of how to be a valuable and congenial part of their social background, without allowing it to condition and overwhelm them.

Take Dennis. He is plainly bright and profitable in his profession. But although he makes such a fine living for them through his business, this is clearly not the complete Dennis. Nothing like the complete Dennis. Evidently, he has an undoubted artistic side, and very striking it can be, too. For instance, he fashions the most wonderful figures of birds and animals from the privet hedges around their terrific home, Carthage. Apparently, he taught himself this topiary skill. It's an amateur pursuit, yes, but one at which Vince and I very much doubt he could be bettered by someone actually in the hedge-trimming trade. I don't think he will be leaving his career in what I understand is insurance broking, but if he did, he could certainly make a living at what is, after all, an authentic art form, and could surely be in demand as suburban development, with its customary privet, spreads under Government plans. Apparently, he generally depicts birds – wonderful, recognisable hawks, buzzards and, above all, the magnificent, proud-necked, wide-tailed peacock, currently on show.

Once or twice I've seen him out there on the stepladder, shaping, sculpting, putting finishing touches, sometimes with automatic clippers, sometimes with a machete-type blade. He told us he changes the creatures periodically. The milkman says that a while ago Dennis had a splendid, leaf-formed stalking cat in front of the Carthage living room, its body wonderfully long, tense and menacing. I think, if the creatures were around our garden instead, I'd get quite upset when he made a change. I'd have grown used to seeing a particular shape as if it were a pet and might grow sad when it disappeared, even though something just as brilliant had replaced it.

What we both – Vince and myself – like especially about Dennis is his modesty – indeed humility. The other day, I happened to walk in front of the Seagraves' house when he was at work on part of his hedge. He at once came down from the stepladder and stood with me, gazing at what he'd been creating – a seagull – and asked whether I thought he had it right. He showed a genuine interest in my opinion; I don't mean any kind of sexual chatting up, but a true curiosity about my view. I asked – very tentatively, I might say; I mean, what do I know about topiary? – whether it might be a little more beakish and fierce, the way gulls around here always appear. They have a kind of raw, majestic superiority. I think I actually used those rather rhetorical words. Possibly behind my words lay a suspicion of mine that Dennis might be by nature too gentle and kindly to capture this savage quality.

At any rate, he immediately brought a pen from his pocket, and said, 'You're entirely right, Kate.' And he did an instant sketch of a gull's head on his wrist. Despite the rough-and-readiness, not to mention the speed, of this drawing, it had everything I was trying to describe. Dennis was truly grateful.

He admitted that he'd sensed there was something wrong about the gull's head, but failed to formulate what it might be. I had defined it for him. He would go straight back up his ladder and make alterations. So he did, and I'm sure that when the seagull is finished it will have a fine, authentic, jutting arrogance. I admit I feel a little proud at having some part in this brilliant piece of art. Yes, I'll definitely call it that – art.

And then, Jill. I don't think Jill has anything to do with the topiary. I believe her main talent, and an immense one, will prove to be for friendship. I hope this does not sound like faint praise after my acclaim for matters as precise and solid as Dennis's insurance occupation and the hedging. I certainly do not intend it that way. Vince and I both have the idea that Jill would be able to form easy bonds with all sorts. We hope we shall soon feel entitled to regard Jill as a fine friend ourselves, and definitely more than a mere neighbour. I know that many others in the Drive also think of Jill as a friend. They must have been won by her warmth and consideration, too. There is a grand vitality to her face; a pretty, even beautiful, aquiline face which, I hear, an amateur artist living nearby wanted to paint. I don't think she has ever sat for him, though. She would probably consider that vanity. This is exactly the kind of unaffected person she is.

4

Dear Mum,

Well, I didn't post the earlier bit after all, but hid it in my knicker drawer.

So, I'll continue! This gets a trifle complicated, I fear. But if you are in touch about your visit to us, you must write to me here at the house – Carthage – not at Mrs AV Ward's, obviously. The point is, this would be merely an ordinary, family letter about arrangements, and one for Dennis also to see, with no danger of comeback. Clearly, it would not be you and I writing on topics needing to stay private from him. So, you could mention things about the arrangements and comments on the weather and routine matters. Nothing *difficult*, though. I think you'll know what I mean when I say *difficult*. If you could address it to both of us – joint, naturally – and refer in conversational yet lively style to his broking work and subjects that interest him, such as the films of Alain Delon, or his topiary. Naturally enough, like any human being, however marginal, he loves to believe there are positive aspects to his personality, the damp cut-out. I don't know how he's turned like this against me. Time is damaging. One hedge is a peacock now, a marvellous wide tail and sort of aristocratic beak. Also, we're getting a seagull. He's really safe and sunny when he talks about these things, and that marvellous old smile glints through. He can look remarkably wholesome then, I don't deny, and this is what possibly attracts women, plus the jauntiness and/or flattery he can switch on.

But, oh, Mother, the terrible, savage thing that happened last week was

Mum, I'm sorry the paper is scrunched up and has a smudge or two, but he came back again sooner than I thought, and moving so damn quietly . . . Well, he does that. He takes lessons from snakes. I had to push it all away, under my clothes once more, and then into the special drawer. Later, I had quite a job getting the ink off my knickers! I've been worried about the letter lying there these last three days, and this is the first safe chance I've had. Oh dear, there's that purple word, 'safe' again – sorry. So, I'm going to close now, not being sure where he is today and wearing those damn trainers.

We are very well and hoping you and Father are well. I know Dennis would want me to send his very best to you, as always. We have been having glorious weather and I think I read your area is already suffering a hosepipe ban. As ever, I suppose we are never satisfied. If it's hot we complain about drought, and if the spring and summer are wet we're not satisfied with that, either! As Dad always says, we must look on the bright side. I know I always try to.

Your loving daughter,
Jill

5

Carthage
Tabbett Drive
Exall DL2 4NG
27 May 2005

My dearest Mother,

I find myself with a few minutes, so can continue where I had to break off my last letter very hurriedly owing to peril. I believe I was discussing the summer weather. Yes, it has already been a really warm one for once, hasn't it? Myself, I consider it wrong to complain. Heaven knows we complain enough when we have wet summer months. We are never satisfied! But plants in the garden have been dying, although it's only May, I must admit. That is upsetting. Perhaps it's even worse in your part of the country. I try to do one big shop per week so as not to be among the shelves too much in the heat. Perhaps you should try this if you find shopping such a trial. Dad might even agree to go with you. Some hope!

This will be a short letter because soon I must get on with one or two essential chores, such as the stairs. We have some people here at the weekend, and everything has to look sparkling. Naturally the stairs get quite a bit of use. We are on parade! Not neighbours. No definitely not. In these weekend get-togethers I think I have come to accept that anything can be regarded as normal as long as both – or all – participants agree, without threats or bullying. Some pleasure can be achieved, I would not deny, through extending boundaries, as it's referred to. And after all, normal is just a word and so relative. All kinds of behaviour regarded as perfectly all right now might have been frowned upon and kept very hushed up a couple of decades ago. This does not mean I would approve of anything vulgar. Decorum and some grace are crucial, and respect for others' bodies, plus a certain tact when what are rather slangily referred to as swap-arounds are taking place. We have good lined blinds and are very careful in all respects not to offend neighbours. They are probably a wee bit curious about events here.

I think I shall do an extensive buffet meal for the Saturday, with many types of meat and fish, plus that iced punch which can be very refreshing. As for music, the Simon and Garfunkle tapes yet again, I think! They are so mellow, and without any of that rather threatening, aggressive noise of present so-called rap music.

I trust you are both well. We are fine. Dennis would certainly like to be remembered to you both and we are jointly looking forward to your visit.

Your loving daughter,
Jill

6

Carthage
Tabbett Drive
Exall DL2 4NG
29 May 2005

Dear Cindy,

Well, I always thought I'd detest school reunions, but now I know I had that *so* wrong! (See, I can do italic now!)

First, though, are you really sure it's OK for me to write to you at your home address? I hope so, so here goes! Things must be very different from what I'm used to at this place. I can't tell you how nice it was to meet you again at the Old Girls' evening after all these years. It made me wish I had attended earlier meetings, but it is often difficult for me to get away, as I mentioned. What was *such* a comfort was to hear from someone of my own age that the things which take place here from time to time are not at all unique. Although I had suspected this, I couldn't be sure until I spoke to Cindy Porter (neé Rayner) late of Florence Nightingale House at Moss Imperial School, now Dr Lucinda Porter, with knowledge of all sorts of lives and carry-ons and recovery of invasive items in the Casualty department.

(Please excuse the handwriting. I have to do this letter fast, and have a little damage to my knuckles and arm, in part my own fault, I must admit, the sod.)

Please do not feel too anxious about me. I thought afterwards that I might have made things in my life sound

11

too dark. Put that down to the sherry. I'm sure I shall be all right. It's worrying, the topiary shears and so on, but I have to believe in my ability always to talk a dark crisis back into a spell of tranquility so, all the gossip and joking at school that used to irritate the staff was not completely wasted! – and I remain certain that no matter what he may suspect he does not 100 per cent know, and he would never push to the ultimate trying to find out unless absolutely forced. Gutlessness is his long suit.

Seeing you brought back memories. I recall the school Lit. and Deb. Society debates on such topics as: 'We only learn from history that men never learn from history.' You were in your element, Cindy, on those occasions, speaking with 100 per cent passion and clarity in the Old Lecture Theatre. Debating was *your* long suit. Such skills are never completely wasted, even if there is little obvious call for them in your chosen profession.

As I said, what I would like to do is ring you some time from a public booth, and possibly we could arrange to meet. I do a big shopping trip every week, and an hour or so stuck on the beginning or end is not missed. Of course, please do not, repeat *not* write here or telephone because of his little ways and so on. The trouble with this place with its damn wall-to-wall carpeting is it's hard to hear him moving about. Beigish mostly.

Well, Cindy, I must close now, because of time. It was grand to hear of your holiday in Biarritz, a spot I've always admired, beloved of Edward VII, I believe. He certainly preferred it to Bognor, about which he said, 'Bugger Bognor!' I'm going to give the carpets a bit of a freshening up with a new, most effective liquid cleaner. Apropos that other nice feature of my life which we spoke of briefly, it's still bringing me some consolation. Isn't the weather wonderful? Some complain about lack of rain, but I feel this is tiresomely ungrateful. Some will always complain, though.

Yours, with many happy school memories,
Jill

12

7

My dearest Mother,

In haste. Well, as ever! I think it would be cleverer if you could put off your visit for a little while. There are some difficulties. But, please, don't worry, just difficulties. You really mustn't, Ma – worry, I mean. It was lovely to read about the new octagonal conservatory, which are so Edwardian and chic. I consider the Edwardians had a lot going for them, and not just Edward VII saying 'Bugger Bognor' when he wanted to go to Biarritz. I've always regarded chicness as your long suit. What I think would be smartest is if you could write to us and say that certain matters have come up at *your* end making a visit in September and October as planned rather tricky. Or you could telephone, since this would be unconfidential material. If you do write, though, this should be one of the joint letters, written here to Carthage for both of us, not sent care of Mrs AV Ward to her address, of course.

So, it would be better if the difficulties you refer to which prevent your coming should *not* be to do with the Edwardian conservatory, because he knows nothing of this, it having been mentioned only in the latest confidential letter to *moi*. Illness would be all right, or redecoration. If you pick illness it should obviously be something serious enough to spoil your plans for several months ahead, yet curable. It would be more effective for you to say you can't come than for me to tell him I think we ought to postpone the invitation because of the difficulties here, liable to continue into the autumn. Otherwise he is going to say in his special, confrontational way, 'What difficulties?' He'd really pretend there were *no* difficulties and certainly none that might last till September or October. This is all part of his damn tactic. Leaving it until the New Year might be the best idea. He is always one to claim there are no difficulties, yet being the whole filthy cause of them. He is going to act unforgiving and hurt when you write to postpone, but that is better than if you and Dad were staying here while difficulties existed, even though part hidden.

How deeply appreciative he was and is of the remarks in your last 'open' letter about the Alain Delon films and his hedge clipping. If you could mention further along those lines it would be beneficial. It makes him feel noticed and worthwhile. There is an Alain Delon film called *Red Sun* which you did not refer to last time and which you could bring up in the next letter. It's a Western but to do with a samurai sword somehow as well, if you could allude to this. But then again, perhaps it would seem unusual if you knew the name of this unfamous film made in 1971, so it might be better if you left it untitled and just wrote vaguely of Alain Delon and the samurai sword, and he will be able to remark in his grand way, 'She means *Red Sun*', and this will build him up temporarily – really, every little helps.

Well, the papers are still full of Iraq, a country at war with itself – always terrible to hear of. Foreign policy has been a problem for so long, hasn't it, Mum? I remember Lord Carrington on TV News meeting mighty snags when trying to sort out Bosnia. Although not young, he had a most effective liquid voice in those days, yet it was not really designed for such things, with gunfire and atrocities everywhere. I don't believe that even he, with that rare voice, could have sorted out Iraq.

Another weekend party last week, with some new people included. This can make things more interesting, obviously, as long as they behave reasonably, though, with stamina spot early what is required. There is an art to 'swinging' it's termed. I hate brashness in physical matters, but, on the other hand, a certain disregard for restraint is a real plus. They were deeply appreciative of a large peach flan. It's a lot of cleaning up, before and after, but I try to look on the bright side.

I'll close now. The weather has turned colder. People who were moaning about the sunshine are now naturally moaning because it's gone. The hedges and his animals and birds are very useful as a screen, of course. He certainly knows about self-protection. Even so, I imagine neighbours notice how the curtains here are kept closed some weekends and wonder. I do feel self-conscious about this to a degree, but the noise is kept quite moderate. I don't consider it inhospitable or fussy to require guests not to groan and cry out like some damn porn video. This regard for decorum and control is in my upbringing, I suppose. Dad always hated indoor noise! Dennis is the same. Never mind, perhaps the summer will pick up again. I know Dennis would wholeheartedly wish to be very warmly remembered to you if he knew I was writing.

Your loving daughter,
Jill

8

Vince and I talk about Jill Seagrave quite a lot. Perhaps it's natural when moving into a new district, as we have, to focus on one, established neighbour. Just the same, neither Vince nor I feel sure we have really caught her

*character, her personality. I'd hate to sell her cheap. So,
what is it I have failed to portray properly? What? What?
I think, perhaps, her energy, vigour, spirit. And I haven't
given her looks full due, either. So, let's put that right first,
it being easier than trying to wrap up someone's essence
as it were.*

*Tall, at least by my standards. Say 5 foot 8 or 5 foot 9.
Slim, and, in fact, almost thin . . . yes, possibly* too *slim,
though never bony and always a combination of elegance
and athleticism. I know I've said aquiline about her face.
That's all right, I suppose, but it's not a term I like all that
much. It makes her sound rather craggy and forbidding.
After all, aquiline does mean like an eagle. An eagle can
certainly be beautiful, but it is in an aloof, chilling, preda-
tory way – the same sort of inherent ferocity as I suggested
to Dennis might be necessary for his hedge seagull. Jill's
features are in no sense like that. They are distinguished,
well-balanced and even, but without being in the least
stand-offish. Hair very fair, perhaps assisted now, though
skilfully done and worn very short – somewhere between
an Eton crop and a pageboy. I'm not sure the style is entirely
right for Jill. Her neck is on show and this might not be
her best feature. But the styling itself is of exceptional flair.
I know it is what she calls 'one of my little extravagances'
to go to London occasionally for a hairdressing session,
as she told us, 'Just like Frank Churchill in* Emma'. *She
seems exceptionally well-read and does know how to use
a reference.*

*Now, does that sound catty? Really, it's not meant to. The
opposite. I envy her this ability to enrich a conversation with
an apt allusion to the classics. And I'm sure she would never
overdo it. Not in her nature. She would regard it as vulgar
to boast of her knowledge.*

*Then, to clothes. Jill certainly knows how to dress. She
has decided what suits her, and has decided well. I suppose
we all think we know what's best for us, but Jill really has
worked out a brilliant style. By this I don't mean that*

everything she wears is top-drawer, expensive, designer stuff. In fact, I see her around in quite inexpensive, casual gear. I mean, cord trousers and an ordinary top, that kind of thing – say, a man's style simple shirt, or, when it's hot, a sleeveless vest-type cotton job. She looks fine like that, easy-going yet crisp, cheerful and approachable. Occasionally, though, she tries colours not absolutely right for her. Blue, for instance, is definitely not Jill. But even when something is wrong for her she can almost make up for it by the animation of her face and social – yes, I'll say it, her social grace. That's not extravagant.

Animation, social grace, perhaps these are the more general qualities that Vince and I have been trying to fathom. It is an animation that is not merely a matter of what appears in her lovely face, though. It is very much her. *And the social grace is not merely something kept for parties and get-togethers but is radiated always from her.*

9

Carthage

Dear Greg,

Can't make it this week, love. Will miss you, miss you, miss you. Just imposs. to get there, though. Will definitely be in touch soonest, or sooner.

Thinking of you,
Jill

10

My dear Mother,

To continue from last week, one really does grieve re. the continuing trouble in Iraq. People 'over there' get no let up. You could be out for a coffee and the person at the next table gets blown up. I've written the envelope to you in advance today as I'm not quite sure of Denn's whereabouts, so if this letter is incomplete it's from necessity. I'll just post it as before to show I'm all right. I don't think I would ever accuse him of not feeling the stress here, too. I would like to repeat that I could love him still if only

11

Carthage
Tabbett Drive
Exall DL2 4NG
Monday

Dear Tim,

I trust you will not mind my bothering you with what could be regarded as a very personal and private matter. Frankly, I have nowhere else to turn. I have put off for some while bothering you, but now I feel unable to continue in this alone.

You will already have deduced in your quick way, I expect, that it is about Jill. There are some things going on which I do not understand at all, and others which, perhaps, I do, and wish I didn't. Please, Tim, think of this letter as like the old days: your younger brother, Dennis, coming for help and advice, which you were always generously willing to give. I suppose I could talk to you about it all on the phone, but I feel more at ease using the word processor, more able to get things explained clearly.

Jill seems to have developed a terrible and, need I say, wholly inexplicable fear of me. I'm sure this will seem absurd to you – as it does to me. You and I both know that I have very precise notions of where violence is permissible, and this would never include against one's wife. Nonetheless, I do sense a continuing dread in her of what I might do. Once or twice when I have come silently to the door of a room – there are fitted carpets everywhere here, deadening sound – I've opened it and found her obviously tensed and straining to hear where I might be in the house, as if, as if Jill is . . . well, the only word is *terrified*, Tim – yes, terrified of being surprised. But why, Tim, why? Once, when leaving the house, I glanced back and caught a look of immense relief on her face as she watched me, part concealed by the upstairs curtains. You can imagine the hurt, even dread, I experienced then.

Possibly your first reaction will be that your kid brother, Dennis, is imagining all this, has suddenly flipped. I could sympathize with such a response, though I do think I can reasonably say that I've almost always been one to keep his feet firmly on the ground. But there is something else. Recently, Tim, I found buried deep in her underwear drawer an uncompleted letter to her mother and father. It was much crumpled and I guessed it had been hurriedly concealed by Jill in her bag or under the clothes she wore at the time, and then transferred to the drawer. Perhaps I'd disturbed her while she was writing. Obviously, Tim, this is not a drawer I would generally, as it were, invade, but I felt such an awful strangeness in the house that I had to try to get to the root of things. Our experience – yours and mine – in that rough business years ago did teach me the value of information. The underwear drawer seemed to me the kind of spot where she might choose to hide sensitive and abusive material because, in the normal course, I would not look there. I decided that, given the grim circumstances, this stratagem was permissible, indeed, imperative. When I looked again later, the letter had gone, of course, presumably completed and sent.

What it said shocked me so much that I transcribed some of the most worrying parts, Tim, and I'm going to include them now, so you can judge independently. She'd plainly had two attempts at the letter and it was how the tacked-on piece ended that upset me most, the sentence broken off, as if she had been surprised for a second time, or simply could not bring herself to go on:

Mother, the terrible, savage thing that happened last
week was

Was what, Tim? What? What? At the time I found the
letter I searched my brain for what in God's name she could
mean, and still don't know. No terrible, savage thing happened
here that I know of. And that is the point, for her letter was
almost entirely about me, the suggestion definitely being that
I had perpetrated this monstrous, whatever it was, on her.
The letter began:

> I would have replied sooner but . . . well, Dennis is in
> and out of the house at odd times and I don't feel safe
> with pen and paper. He notices. It's all right this after-
> noon. He has definitely gone to town, and I would hear
> the car early enough . . .

Now, Tim, perhaps you will begin to understand fully
my disquiet. The letter lays out in relentless detail ways of
communicating secretly, and then descends to a note of
outright hatred and contempt for me. Having referred slight-
ingly to my interest in certain films and topiary, it continues:

> He loves to believe there are various positive aspects
> to his personality, the damp cut-out.

I am at a complete loss as to why she should describe me
in this tone, and I set her thoughts out here in the hope that
you will be able to give a detached but understanding insight
into what you believe has happened between us.

Of course, I have already considered the obvious, that my
Jill, as I used to call her, with no fear of contradiction, yes,
that my Jill has found someone else, and therefore feels not
only a cruel loss of affection towards me, but guilt causing
her to fear I might seek revenge. It would hurt me intoler-
ably if I found for certain she was unfaithful, yet it is a
possibility I know I have to face. But even if such a dreadful

supposition were proved to be fact – incontrovertibly proven – I trust that I would not turn my sorrow and rage to violent revenge. It is one of the most wounding elements in the whole situation that Jill does not seem to know me, and fails to understand my nature even after so long together in such seeming harmony and love. I hope – and believe – that you and I, Tim, have learned enough about the harsh results of violence never to indulge in it lightly again.

Would it be too much to ask, Tim, to tell me how these matters strike you?

Yours,
Dennis

12

Carthage
Tabbett Drive
Exall DL2 4NG
8 June 2005

Dear Tim,

Thanks so much for your prompt, long reply. I knew you would not let me down. I am all the more grateful, dear brother, because I realize your natural instinct is to telephone, not write, but you'll understand it would be awkward to receive that kind of call here, or through the switchboard at work.

No, there have been no further developments that I know of, simply the continuance of this awful, stifling tension. I understand completely that you must ask what you call hard questions and make possibly 'distasteful' suggestions. I want you to be totally frank, as ever. I expected no less when I wrote to you. I still have the feeling that all my movements around the house or in the garden are anxiously monitored by Jill, as though I were a dangerous intruder. This is all the more baffling because in the incomplete letter I found she referred to me as 'yellow deep down' and incapable of anything she called major. What she meant by that I do not know, and do not wish to. But it makes her obvious fear of me so hard to explain.

No, I am not at all offended by your proposal that in the matter of possible infidelity by Jill I should try to follow her, or employ someone to follow her. I had already considered this, as a matter of fact. And, of course, you are right, if it were indisputably proved that she were having another relationship, her bizarre behaviour would be completely accounted for. Snooping is not the kind of action one would wish to take against one's wife, obviously, but, then, an illicit affair is not the kind of action she should pursue, either, surely, Tim? One does not wish to, as it were, score points in this kind of situation, but there has to be some kind of parity of treatment, I feel.

Again no, I have not come across any further correspondence in her underwear drawer, nor have I discovered anything else there that might signal unacknowledged extramarital sexual activity. Yes, I have been very thorough in my searches, unpleasantly furtive as this has to be, as you say.

Your question about the possibility of intercepting letters from her parents in an attempt to deduce what else she has said to them arises from a misunderstanding on your part, I'm afraid – one for which I blame myself. I should have told you in more detail how she and they manage their correspondence. No letters about what she would call *difficult* matters come to this address. They go to a neighbour's, and I have no opportunity to see them, either openly or in secret. We do get letters from her parents, but these are on formal or trivial matters only, and I think Jill instructs them in what to write. Her mother and father were due to have visited us in the coming autumn, for instance, but wrote to cancel, giving some absurd excuse about her mother's duties in the

Oxfam shop. I telephoned several Oxfam shops near where they live and found that none knew Jill's mother. No, I believe Jill asked her parents to call off because of the situation here. It is especially worrying that she should apparently foresee that situation continuing until the autumn. Getting worse? The letters that come here for us jointly throw a deliberate veil over things. They discuss Iraq and the weather, and inquire *so* politely about my interests, obviously humouring me. Yes, they are briefed by Jill, I'm sure. One letter referred with mock vagueness to that obscure Alain Delon film *Red Sun*. Clearly, they wanted to flatter me by giving me the chance to identify the film from a very skimpy description. It is almost impossible that her parents should know of *Red Sun* – vaguely or at all. You can see the lengths to which Jill will go to hoodwink and manipulate her husband. Tim, is this tolerable?

Naturally, I understand entirely that you needed to ask about our sex lives, since this could be an indication of whether she is having a relationship elsewhere. I have to say, sex has not been satisfactory for some while, neither in frequency nor intensity of response by Jill. Oddly, she declares in her letter that she *could* still love me if only I would remain what she calls *sunny* for a matter of weeks. I really fail to fathom this. I think I am how I've always been, how most of us are – a mixture of moods, but never evil.

If you can bear to analyze these rather rambling remarks and let me have your views again, I would be for ever grateful, Tim.

Yours,
Dennis

13

Dear Tim,

I have to say I dislike the tone of your last letter, just arrived. There are wise points in it, of course, but, reading between the lines, I feel you are really saying that what is happening is in some way my fault. In other words, you are adopting the very same negative attitude as she has and turning away from the perils that may exist here. You seem to imply that I have been cold and devoid of understanding. Not true. Oh, not true, Tim. One has tried so hard.

I should not have troubled you. It was probably foolish to expect your understanding when you are so far away and preoccupied with your own problems, no doubt. Forgive me. I shall not write on these matters again.

Yours,
Dennis

14

My dear Ma,

What a fret it is that there's still no proper peace in Iraq. Can we really believe that despite all these incidents progress towards reconciliation does continue? The mix of religions is quite a problem in my view. Mr Bush is a Bible Belt person, I believe, but this might not be of much use when it comes to mosques. We're told people are working away behind the scenes all the time, seeking to create a constitution that will have something for everyone out there, but many will think it has more for others than for them, and then there will be difficulties.

Things go much better here, though, I'm happy to report and I certainly think it will be fine for you and Father to visit in a little while. To pick one word to describe Dennis at this time, I would say serene. I expect this comes as a surprise to you, remembering his sweats and purplings up, but, watching him, I see a sort of exhaustion and a wish for peace, as in Northern Ireland. It is times like these that remind me of how fine he used to be once, that little way he used to sing the main *Messiah* numbers, for instance, talking of religion. All that sweet old semi-holy stuff with its cheerful, positive message for the most part. Now, in the summer, he has his topiary to engage him, and the cinema club is active, too, despite the call of the open air. And I think he must have struck up a correspondence with his brother, for I see letters arriving with the Scottish postmark. They are not usually in touch, so this is a good sign – a means of widening up his mouselike personality and giving it a nice little morale boost. Obviously, he does not leave these letters about, and his brother can be quite quirky and know-all.

I don't wish to sound boastful – if only because it would be tempting fate! – but I think the reason for the change in him is that I have been able to strike a nice balance at these weekend things we have, and in other more private activities. It's tricky. If I show too much zest at our weekend sessions he grows negative, protesting afterwards about how I can be so giving, and asking where I learned such tricks and sustained intensities. Honestly, you would think he had never had the benefit of them himself, and in these weekend things openness and the desire to expand experience are what it's all about, for heaven's sake! It's a dark, resentful show by Dennis, as if everyone should be as tame as leaf peacocks. I have to try to explain to him that the object of these parties is pleasure and that pleasure requires enthusiasm, invention, liberality.

But, on the other hand, Mother, if I act tired or disgusted, that's wrong too, and I'm 'inhospitable', and 'prudish' and 'quasi-frigid'. Lately, though, I think I've got it right – due avidity with the occasional nausea squall. Squall?

Well, isn't the weather astonishingly settled for a British summer, broken only by the occasional shower? We have some brilliant mornings which fill one with true zest. As for my approaching birthday, I dread it, of course. He can grow so foully and creatively vindictive then, picking presents for me certain to cause revulsion. These take an unstinting amount of imaginative thought, I know, such as garments that make me look hideous, the colours most likely copied from therapy paintings by schizos. I have to go about in these lurid rags for weeks, so as to be appreciative and not hurtful. Buying for *his* birthday or Christmas, with his miserable little collection of interests, is hard – alcohol being very unwise, naturally, even ginger wine. And he's got more than enough topiary tools, thank you very much indeed!

Clearly, the surrender of arms by the paramilitaries is essential to the peace process in Northern Ireland, yet perhaps one can understand the reluctance on both sides to leave themselves unprotected. It is a tradition going far back for the IRA that they do not give up arms. It is truly against the grain. Negotiators have to be aware of these feelings and yet still press on for the permanent end to hostilities which, surely, almost everyone in that ravaged island craves. I'm going to close now, hoping that you are both well. I know Dennis would want to send his very best wishes, with thanks for the remarks about the Delon film, which I am sure he found timely and constructive.

Your loving daughter,
Jill

15

Carthage
Tabbett Drive
Exall DL2 4NG
9 June 2005

Dear Cindy,

I'm just writing a formal line to say how delighted Dennis and I were to be welcomed into your lovely home on Tuesday. You certainly keep your home beautifully, and we were both extremely impressed by Julian and his wittiness. I hope you and I did not tire the men with our endless talk of school days! I can't tell you what a treat it is for me to be a guest in someone's home when my usual personal outings are more informal. I know Dennis was quite sincere in his offer to create a creature of interest and majesty in your hedge. He thinks of a hedge as like a cage from which his art can free some hidden creature. This is a genuine flair and I think he was born up a stepladder.

Our journey home was without incident, despite heavy rain the whole distance. The journey seemed to pass very rapidly and we happily discussed the time we had spent with you and Julian. We were almost unaware of the unseasonal weather lashing against the car and hindering vision.

We certainly both hope you will be able to return the visit to our home very soon. I expect you will agree with us that the continuing rows in the Conservative party over Europe are both foolish and sad. It's no wonder that Sir Edward Heath became fretful towards the end of his life, since he was the architect of so much of this country's positive attitude to Europe, and yet he kept his voice quite temperate occasionally. Far back in his career he used to work for the *Church Times*, or something like that, which was an Anglican paper, but this did not put him off Europe, despite its many Catholic countries. Some weekends we have people in for a pleasant time socialising and so on. We both feel you would enjoy their company and know they would enjoy yours. That goes without saying! At these get-togethers music is of a mild, even subdued, nature, which I feel certain would be to your and Julian's taste – and parking is no problem. I'd enjoy hearing your views of our guests, and Julian's witty views in all respects. These occasions are of a quite *informal* nature. Myself, I've come to terms with much of it and one can't worry for ever about health. In any case, as a doctor, you would probably have any necessary antidotes at your fingertips.

Well, I'll close now, wishing to hear the lates on the news re the Middle East, which seems to be endlessly grim. I know Dennis would wish me to send his very best wishes and his thanks again for a lovely, polished evening.

Your good friend,

Jill

16

Carthage

Dear Greg,

Sunday will be fine, thank God, thank God. Same place. Was that you who rang here, pretending to be double glazing when he answered? Wow! So resourceful!

J

17

Carthage
Tabbett Drive
Exall DL2 4NG
Tuesday

Dear Mother,

A brief word because he's not being too reliable again lately and my handwriting might turn jumpy. If he ever gets in direct touch with you, being wily and so on, trying to find out etc, just play it dead blank, won't you, with absolute ignorance of anything *difficult*? Well, I know you are reliable and I don't need to say this, most probably. Who shops their own kid?

However, it occurred to me, that's all, that he might try a head-on approach to you. He can be artful. Obviously, no mention, please, of Mrs AV Ward, who has been in her Veronica, not Alice, state these last few days, which does damage to nobody. She wears cravats and chunky bangles when Veronica, and makes her smiles more forceful and engulfing. In another historical period he would have been quite near the normal; I always say that for him. Think of the Vandals. Dennis would have done nicely in that savage, ancient tribe – who were eventually defeated at Carthage, as a matter of fact! The summer continues brilliantly, doesn't it? He is quite tanned in his little way.

Dennis, I know, would wish me to convey his very best and to encourage you to take advantage of the fine weather while it is still here!! I must close now for safety.

Your loving daughter,
Jill

18

Carthage

Dear Greg,

Darling, you might be right, after all. I was watchful on the way home and did get the impression of a car sticking with me, tailing right to the house. Of course, I was tense after what you'd said about possible private eye agents, and I could have been imagining. It's often tricky to sort out what's real from what is cooked up in one's head. Then again, we see so much of this kind of snooping in TV drama that it's easy to grow jumpy. Anyway, I stayed watchful and got the impression of one man alone in the car behind. It passed the house when I stopped.

As you said recently, all we hear about is the debate on our licensing laws and the proposed changes. There are certainly points for and against. I'll say this, Greg, he is capable of such drab behaviour as putting a gumshoe on to me. I don't mean he would do it himself, and it was not Denn in the car, I'm sure, a Ford Finesse. He is the sort who'd employ someone for this smelly task, however, and receive full, confidential reports. Some women might feel it a compliment that he should care enough. My mother would say so, but she does not have to witness his smiles or nail cleaning.

Darling, I find I can't worry very much about it. My head is full of the loveliness of our time together on Sunday – visions of our future, the happy talk, grand, prestige labels on your garments, the sweet brutalities and distinguished clarets. I love the sounds we make, so uninhibited. Obviously, I have had certain experiences, which I never tried to conceal, yet there is always a seeming newness about the lovely times with you. He says nothing, noting departure and arrival. Occasionally he refers to the continuing danger to the peace process in Northern Ireland, which is certainly real, as if this was the only matter preoccupying him, though it's hard to imagine him sincere about anything. Don't get me wrong, he has very sound aspects, and in another time and overseas conditions he would probably be acceptable and entirely unthreatening. I must close.

All my love, as you know,

Your Jill

19

*Y*ou'll be asking why I'm so preoccupied by the Seagraves.
If I'm not careful it's going to look as if I have a bit of
a pash for one or other of them. Or even both. Was there
some breathlessness in the way I described Jill, her beauty,
elegance, social talents? Have I gone overboard for Dennis's
artistic skills, as seen in the topiary birds and animals? Well,
I am fond of them, fond of them both, but I honestly don't
think it's in that way, not towards either of them.

No, the point is a rumour went around that they were
thinking of selling up and moving elsewhere. I have to say,
it might be only rumour. I haven't spoken to Jill or Dennis
about it, and there is no For Sale notice, as far as I can see.
It's not something I feel one should ask them about. If they
want to tell me, they will tell me. I don't know where the
tale started, but two or three people have mentioned it to
me – have actually asked me if I knew whether it were true.

I think it's the possibility they might go from Tabbett Drive
that has made me realize how much I value their presence
here. I think others have felt the same. And so I've tried to
work out why in some detail, and that's what I have been
writing here. Quite apart from everything else, I cannot
imagine how Dennis would be willing to leave the hedges
on which he has done so much splendid and sensitive work.
I suppose that might sound a trivial point, but I admit it
struck me very powerfully when I first heard the rumours.

I cannot totally dismiss these stories, unfortunately. I have
to say, I have noticed a kind of restlessness in Jill lately. It is
something generally very well hidden by her affability and

charm. But, yes, I have been aware of it once or twice. We can all suffer boredom, can't we? Jill might not be immune to that, despite the brilliant interest she always shows in people close to her, and in the world and its goings on generally. I have had the feeling now and then that she is looking around, not content with her setting any longer. Perhaps she feels tired of Tabbett Drive. Perhaps Dennis does, too. Or possibly he wishes to stay. It might be a delicate topic, which would be why we are still at only the rumour stage – and why it would be unwise to ask them straight out if they intend to move on.

I would certainly miss them. And I hope I have given a convincing explanation of why that is so.

20

Carthage
Tabbett Drive
Exall DL2 4NG
14 June 2005

Dear Ma and Pa,

How lovely of you it was to remember our wedding anniversary and to send such a lovely gift. Dennis was truly thrilled, as I was myself, naturally. I feared you might forget, yet did not wish to remind you, in case I seemed pushy! We had a happy though restrained celebration of our wondrous years together, the kind of occasion you both would have enjoyed, I'm sure.

This celebration took the delightful form of a pleasant meal in one of our most favourite and, indeed, most friendly restaurants, namely Alvin's Bistro. We are well known there and Alvin in person always comes to our table for a pleasant chat during the meal. He does not lay on the foreignness, like some of them – all that 'Bon soir, madame' stuff – yet does look French, or maybe Spanish, in a perfectly suitable way for a restaurant. Myself, I see no harm in the very tight trousers they wear, as long as this does no lasting harm or makes them spill stuff – the food, I mean, of course! Fortunately, the weather turned to a nice coolness, quite different from the scorching sun that prevailed on our actual wedding day, that everyone concerned must remember! But it did not seem of importance at the time, of course. Nothing could have spoiled that joyous occasion.

The build-up to my birthday, plus the anniversary, make this a very difficult period full of pain and insult, but getting out to somewhere conducive such as Alvin's Bistro is in many ways a remedy and we both thrill at what he does to veal, fortunately. This comes with a crême sauce, yet not heavy, and bearing a faint but sufficient winey taste, also. Alvin knows our joint(!) preference for this dish and has it written down on his pad almost before we've stated our order! He sensed that it was indeed a special occasion for us and brought complimentary glasses of that drink which the Italians set on fire in a small glass! It really was quite a sight, and somehow wonderfully apt for a special occasion. There are times I'd love to torch Dennis. It would be unrealistic to expect him to go through an anniversary day and celebratory meal devoid of all alcohol, and I am happy to say that admirable sleepiness took him over before we left for home.

Naturally, there was some evil when we reached there, some stocktaking of the years, yet all within decent limits, more or less, and total respect for your gift, which will have a place of honour, believe me. For desert I had that wondrous item, a *zabaglione*, while Dennis, as ever, opted for vanilla ice cream – always venturesome, the piffling jerk. Oh, I have not mentioned the starters, a special feature at Alvin's, and he would be hurt! I had their wondrous minestrone, full of fresh vegetable fragments, and Dennis, as is customary for him, opted for the hors d'oeuvre, which are really extensive.

I believe it's important to mark these anniversaries regardless of current acute menace. Such occasions look forward as well as into the past, I always feel.

It might be wisest if you put the matter of a visit 'on the back burner' as they say. He is very taken up with the topiary at present, in a pleasant, fulfilling fashion. If he decides to change the peacock etc, I will let you know what the replacements are, because he likes people to recognize at once what he's done and can get a bit evil over mistakes. It's a lot of work for him, up and down the stepladder, needing to step back to get a proper perspective, because close up, when you are cutting it, a hedge is just a hedge, of course, and you have to stand away to see whether it is a peacock or cheetah.

Well, I must close now. I decided to write this one in the reading room of the public library for safety, so he's not nosing, and they are about to close. Fortunately the coolness still holds admirably, and I shall enjoy the little stroll to the car now.

Your loving daughter,
Jill

21

Fairholm
Tabbett Drive
Exall DL2 5NG
14 June 2005

RD Simms
UN Emergency Force
PO Box 71
Central Africa

My dear Rowena,

Hi, Ro, your sister Alice (or sometimes Veronica) calling. Hope this reaches you. It feels like dropping a letter into nowhere. I mean, such an address – not exactly precise. Just how it must have been if someone wanted to send a line to Mr Kurtz in *Heart of Darkness*. But I expect you move about as the terrible effects of this appalling famine show themselves in different spots. Naturally, I follow it all on TV, hoping to catch sight of you one day behind the wheel of a supply truck, and among all those suffering bodies. It's great that you can phone me now and then, but I quite see it's impossible the other way.

So, how can I compete in the way of news from the depths of Bourgeoisville here? Things proceed in their sleepy way. But we do seem to have a 'situation' a little way up the road – no names or address, in case this letter goes astray. My lady neighbour has some nasty, though so far unspecified, problems, I fear. I see quite a bit of her because she uses me as a 'poste restante', being fearful of letters going to her own home in case they are opened by her hubbie. That will give you some idea of her plight – in fact, as much of an idea as I have myself, despite some subtle, I hope, questioning. Not subtle enough to prise anything out of her to date. I think it's a legitimate curiosity, if she is truly in danger.

Actually, this is hard to accept because her husband is really quite a dish, and friendly with it. In fact, sometimes when I'm in what you'd call 'one of those Veronica moods', I dream of . . . but enough, enough! These are coarse, heated fantasies. He's too young, anyway. Or, putting it another, crueller, way, I'm too ancient. (Ancient enough to be whispered about for the OBE, but keep this under your sun hat.) Strange events there at some weekends, I think – lots of cars, music, drawn curtains. Eric and I get no invite – again.

So, you see, perhaps things are not all that sedate and banal here, after all. Do guard yourself, darling, and keep taking the tablets. Will let you know of any further excitements on my little patch.

Much love,
Alice

22

Carthage
Tabbett Drive
Exall DL2 4NG
16 June 2005

Dear Anna,

I'm so glad we parted friends and kept in touch despite everything! Frankly, I need some advice. It's urgent. I've tried my brother, Tim, but he has his own strange way of looking at things, as I expect you remember. It struck me just now that what I really want is a woman's point of view – if you can spare a moment, lounging by your pool. But hang on, I suppose it might be autumn or winter down there, if South Africa *has* a winter!

It's about Jill, yes. Let me say at once that I can guess what you think – that I knew what I was taking on with Jill, so why squeal. I understand this reaction – really! But, as you appreciated better than anyone, I was on the rebound, and a bit haywire at the very least, dear Anna.

I expect you think you understood her pretty well, and I thought I did. I'm not blaming you at all. Now, I fear, I can't tell what she is capable of. Her eyes are hellishly mobile, but rarely setting on me. Sitting with her in some fancy cafe for our anniversary, and behaving totally marital and constructive, I watch her send her dangerous mind in all directions but where I am, Anna. Yet this is supposed to be a celebration of *our*, yes *our*, anniversary. She shows what I can only describe as contempt for these many shared years, and it's something you would never do. The Boer, your new man, is lucky.

Jill's got someone else. I don't mean just something casual – gratification. That would be merely par for the course. No, this is damn solid and long-lasting. They have been observed – all the usual carry-on, which I need not describe, I think. Never, ever, do I contemplate violence, regardless. All that kind of thing is in the past and must remain there. Must. My reason for writing to you is to ask what I can do to reach her, in your view. What should I say, do? My identity is diminished, or will be, unless I act. *You* left me, *she* is leaving me and fears me. She will wish to guard herself against me, as she in her poisoned way would see it, guard herself by any means. You know what she is capable of, dear Anna. But perhaps you think it odd, a cheek, that I should ask your advice on such a matter in view of our previous closeness. That is all a long while ago, though, and I hope you will be kind and generous now.

Tell me, tell me, for God's sake, why I alienate women who have loved me. A certain amount of hired and professional prying was necessary to reveal matters, but I assure you this is not my customary behaviour. I found some of her letters she writes in the public library among dossers and tramps. This is the crisp, brilliantly avid girl I wedded? Help me, do.

In continuing friendship,
Dennis

23

Carthage
Tabbett Drive
Exall DL2 4NG
16 June 2005

My dear Tim,

It was very – and typically – decent of you to send the anniversary card, despite my last foolishly hostile letter to you. The verse on the card was hopeful – inspiringly hopeful, without being too gushing. I'm glad you addressed it to both of us, it being very well received by Jill.

I think that with professional aid I've identified him, though not someone I know. Inquiries at his work and in the neighbourhood indicate he is passably respected. Jill would be quite capable of securing someone like that: she can act whatever part is needed. There must be more to it than mere lust. This kind of more profound relationship would be so in character for Jilly, of course. She is unable to countenance anything casual, except in special circumstances.

Confused and pained, naturally, I have written to Anna Bates, as she was, seeking advice. I know you and I both esteemed Anna in our different ways, an endearingly responsive girl. Possibly, you were closer to her longer than I, though I thought you would not mind if I tried to contact her about my problems, especially as she is now married. She always had a way of summing things up, and she and Jill shared many social outings and so on, when they were younger. Anna will have some knowledge of Jill's leanings, though probably not impartial. Yet all information has its uses.

I don't think we are yet near a crisis and, while greatly appreciating your offer to visit, I feel this might not be advantageous just now. In its greasy, approximate way, our anniversary celebration did achieve something, I believe, causing Jill to see the continuities of life, rather than its episodes, often untidy. Your card and others, feelingly displayed, gave colour to this idea of durability, stability and the sweetly sacramental. I certainly felt better for it all and am sure we shall reach our next anniversary in at least as good shape, regardless.

Yours,
Dennis

24

27 Perdita Close
Amberchase
Lancs
16 June 2005

Dear Mrs Ward,

As Jill Seagrave's mother, I have increasingly felt of late that I should address a note to you – I mean to you, personally, not 'care of Mrs AV Ward'. This has always seemed strange, writing to you, yet not, since Jill is the real recipient. I am grateful for the help you give her, and me. I know she will already have thanked you, and she repeatedly speaks well of you in her letters. But I wish to acknowledge your kindness personally.

In addition, I would like to discuss a point about Jill, if I may. She has always been a rather imaginative person and, in fact, *very* imaginative, even fanciful. I wonder sometimes whether the precautions she insists on for my mail to her are necessary. Perhaps you, too, think it a little weird and far-fetched. All the more credit to you, then, for going along with Jill's arrangements, particularly when I'm sure you are busy enough with your own life. You see, Mrs Ward, some of the things Jill says or hints at in letters to us about her husband bear hardly any resemblance to my own and Jill's father's impressions of Dennis. Of course, we view things from the outside and are dependent on such information as Jill sends. Nobody can be certain what takes place privately between those in a marriage. Dennis always struck us as an exemplary, warm-hearted, balanced figure, of fine background, devoted to Jill and determined to make a good life for the two of them, and for children should those come along. Have things changed so much that the reflections on him made by Jill week after week now are justified? We would dearly like to visit, to find out for ourselves, but Jill is adamant that we come only when she considers it 'right'. This seems to be never.

I would be very glad, when you have a moment, if you could drop me the briefest of lines to say whether, as a trusted neighbour, you have ever observed anything actual and real that would account for Jill's anxieties and fears.

Yours sincerely,
Gwen Day (Mrs)

25

Carthage
Tabbett Drive
Exall DL2 4NG
17 June 2005

Dear Mr Lavery,

I wish to say how pleased I am with the way Mr Nelmes has conducted the inquiries for which I engaged your private detection company, re my wife Mrs Jill Seagrave. I am happy to enclose a cheque as interim payment, as you request. I am, let me assure you, Mr Lavery, most appreciative of the delicacy with which Mr Nelmes has carried out what must have been a distasteful task, and of the sensitive yet full manner in which he has composed his reports. Never could they be comfortable reading, obviously, yet he has contrived to be at once graphic (but not pornographic), unambiguous and tactful. I congratulate him and your company.

I hope he will be able to continue in the assignment for a little while yet. This is not merely a matter of possible evidence for a court hearing, but the acquiring of information to which, quite simply, I feel wholly entitled as a husband, and mean to have. I am sure your man has instructions to reveal nothing of who has employed him, should he ever be discovered and challenged. Mrs Seagrave can be very sharp and very combative. The client's anonymity would no doubt be an understood principle by a firm of your considerable professional repute, but I would be grateful for a formal confirmation by return. And, of course, I would not wish this letter, nor any part of it, to be used by you as an endorsement advertising your services. Again, I am sure there is no need for me to spell this out. The skill with which you and Mr Nelmes have handled this task is heartwarming, since it would distress me greatly if I thought my wife were aware of being observed and so felt threatened. It is obviously my prime aim to continue to treat her only with proper regard.

Yours sincerely,
DW Seagrave

26

Fairholm
17 June 2005

RD Simms
UN Emergency Force
PO Box 71
Central Africa

My dear Rowena,

Although your part of the world seems to have dropped out of our news, I'm sure it does not mean those appalling problems have been resolved.

It seems rather absurd and selfish of me in the circumstances to be bringing you my small-scale worries, but they are in the front of my mind and, in any case, what else do I write about: Eric's bloody golf, Eric's bloody car, Eric's bloody health?

I've now had a letter from the mother of the neighbour I mentioned more or less asking me if I think her daughter has gone mad. I don't know how to reply. I've tried a couple of times, but gave up. Perhaps she is – mad I mean, imagining all sorts of dangers from her husband. Persecution mania? I think I'll write back as if this question has never been raised and discuss safe generalities instead. This will take care of politeness and avoid sensitive areas.

My indecisiveness is made worse because I've bumped into the husband a couple of times lately in the Drive and, really, I cannot associate him with the kind of person implied by his wife's fears and her craving for secrecy. Frankly, Ro, he's a charmer, and in other circumstances . . . by 'other circumstances' I mean Eric, of course, plus the fact that this very desirable neighbour is married to a friend. All that apart, I find it impossible to see him in the kind of terror role that my neighbour claims. I must say, he does seem to have taken rather a shine to me.

If I tell the mother that I believe her daughter's exaggerating, or even imagining it totally, the mother will be pleased to think her daughter's safe – as I'm sure she is – but worried in case she has become deranged. Eric is unhappy about the whole business of taking in post for the neighbour. Well, naturally, knowing Eric! He'd prefer to have as little to do with her as possible, owing to his suspicions of what goes on at their house some weekends. He stresses the need for me to keep my nose clean because of the OBE possibility. He says he's sure there *are* swingers who have the OBE and even peerages, but it would be silly to invite risk 'at this juncture'. That's one of Eric's regular phrases, 'at this juncture'. He's a 'not at this juncture' sort of person. I don't know what he would do if we got an invitation. At least, I do know. Eric would refuse. But me? There might be something to be said for meeting the husband under such conditions, whatever they might be. Regrettably, it seems to me, though, that the Carthage couple never invite close neighbours.

So, you see, Ro, life here is not without its little dramas. Take care.

All my love,
Veronica (today)

27

Carthage
Tabbett Drive
Exall DL2 4NG
UK
27 June 2005

Dear Anna,

It was a real tonic in my present anxious state to receive your letter. Of course, she is intrigued by airmail from South Africa but I definitely got there first and she had no chance to open it and do a nose. It's coming up to her birthday; an occasion I always dread, because of her terrible ingratitude over gifts. For myself, I have always looked forward to others' birthdays and to Christmas. One takes great pleasure in selecting presents. It's that subtle combination of choices, arising out of what one wishes to give the recipient and what one feels the recipient would wish for themselves – a challenging matter of achieving a balance.

As you say, it is a deeply distressing coincidence that you should be suffering the same kind of rejection and possible heartless betrayal in your adopted country that I undergo here. I can't say how much it grieves me to hear of your pain, dear Anna. Oh, could we but put the clock back those years and have the chance to rectify such terrible mistakes. I don't mean the appalling violence we were forced into – and I feel utterly entitled to say forced – but the separations that followed. I experience some guilt about presenting you with my problems, when you have so many of your own, though, of course, I did so out of ignorance of your plight, and out of dire need. And yet, despite your own pain, you find time to offer me consolation and advice. This is so typical of the Anna I knew. In a way it thrills me to hear that you may return to this country, although the reasons are so sad. It would be truly wonderful to see you again.

Of course, you are wholly right, there must come a time very soon when I confront Jill with my suspicions – indeed, my certainties. It is so typically forthright of you to say so, and so typically brave of you to have done the same in your own circumstances. On the other hand, you are also entirely right to suggest that this is certainly no matter for wild vindictiveness or revenge, reactions which you can rest assured I have learned, from that earlier experience, are utterly unproductive long-term. We are not Sicilians, obsessed by vendettas, I hope!

Would I could offer you, in return, some similar helpful advice, though you do not seem to need this, having faced your problem and dealt with it. All I will say is that you can rely on me for every support should you do as you are contemplating and come 'home'. Although in contact with Tim again, I will not mention to him that you may soon be in Britain. I think this is wisest in view of how things turned out last time. He can be so destructive and sour, though in many ways fine most of the time.

Please keep me in touch with your plans.

Yours ever,
Dennis

28

Memo:
Date: 27 June 2005
From: Susan Wright (counsellor)
To: Catherine Wilberforce (supervisor)

At our next tutorial I would like to discuss with you the case of Mrs AVW and I am forwarding a summary of my notes on this client so that you will be au fait.

She first came to us for marriage guidance about four months ago and I have seen her four or five times since at irregular intervals. She is uncomfortable with the notion that she might need counselling – ashamed, I think – and on each occasion I have seen her she has told me this would be her final visit. But after some weeks she will telephone the office to make a further appointment. She says she discloses to nobody that she comes here, and insists there is no question of asking her husband to accompany her. She is evidently averse to what she would probably regard as dependency.

She is forty-three, in a very responsible Civil Service post and, she tells me, possibly in line for some kind of honours award, such as an OBE. Her husband, E, is the same age, a successful businessman. There is a daughter of thirteen away at boarding school.

For a long time she has felt neglected in her marriage. Her husband, she says, is preoccupied with his work and with golf, and has little time for her. She claims he is also a hypochondriac. Their sex life is virtually defunct. She says that she has contemplated leaving, but is bound by all the

48

usual restraints: the child, lifestyle and a dread of scandal, in view of her professional and social positions.

She says she feels isolated and fears she might be driven into clinical depression by her own indecisiveness. (Clearly, she is capable of profound self-analysis.) She says she is so conscious of a duality in herself that she will sometimes prefer to be called by her first name and sometimes by her middle name, depending on her 'mood' at the time. She has a sister working abroad, whom she keeps in touch with, and to whom, in some degree, she opens her heart; though not so far as to admit that she is being counselled. There is a younger woman neighbour with whom she has established a significant friendship: our client has agreed to receive some of this woman's mail for her, so that her (the neighbour's) husband will not see it.

My early interviews with Mrs AVW were, of course, designed to lead her to define fully for herself and me her attitude to the marriage, with the aim of eventually removing the indecisiveness which she regards as potentially so damaging. That is, I wished to take her to a point where she would frankly evaluate the gains and losses in staying or going and make a definite choice. Although she remained uncertain, these early interviews were comparatively simple because she appeared to have no sexual interest in anyone outside the marriage. It was only a matter of whether she wanted to stay with E.

This has now changed and she finds herself attracted lately to the husband of the woman neighbour for whom she acts as poste restante. She believes he might be attracted to her. For several reasons she is apprehensive about this potential relationship:

1. The man is much younger than herself.
2. She is a friend of his wife and feels a loyalty to her, especially given the closeness implied by the secret postal stratagem.
3. Because of her work with the Police Authority and the possibility of a decoration, she fears scandal.
4. In view of the wife's apparent fear of her husband, our

client is worried that she (the client) might be mistaken in finding him worthwhile. Although she suspects that the wife is imagining dangers where there are none, she is by no means certain of this.

Our client sees that in some ways the development of this attraction to the neighbour's husband might force her (Mrs AVW) towards the decisiveness she feels she needs, and recognizes this could be an eventual psychological advantage. At the same time, her attitude towards the neighbour's husband is itself attended by new uncertainties and additional elements of indecisiveness. I feel that I might be picking up some of the confusion and would like input from you on the best way to direct counselling with her in the future, supposing she returns.

SW
27 June 2005

29

Fairholm
Tabbett Drive
Exall DL2 5NG
27 June 2005

Dear Mrs Day,

Thank you very much for your kind letter about your daughter, Jill. Please believe it is no inconvenience to me and my husband to receive letters for her here. As they say, what else are neighbours for? In fact, the arrangement has been a real boon, giving me more opportunities than I might otherwise have had to chat with her. I can assure you that she revels in your letters and is always full of joy when she has recently read one. To witness this joy is more than enough reward for the small service of providing an accommodation address. It is certainly not for me to show undue inquisitiveness about the reasons for Jill's behaviour, I'm sure you'll agree. Have no hesitation in writing here, Mrs Day, and perhaps we shall meet one day when you visit Jill.

Yours sincerely,
Alice V Ward

30

Carthage
Tabbett Drive
Exall DL2 4NG
27 June 2005

My dear Mother,

Despite the supposed health of the economy under Mr Brown, many firms still go to the wall because people are not spending enough. They fear an economic collapse. The Iraq situation sounds just as bad as ever. Nobody can foresee an end. I think that if I were Mrs Blair I'd be quite worried about my husband's level of stress, having to keep a full dental smile on regardless of failures and lampooning. This is supposing she's fond of him, obviously, which I'm sure she is, otherwise it might please her. Some ministers working for Blair seem pretty terrible. I call that very tough one with all the grey gelled hair 'the schmuck of firm government'.

I happened to come across what Denn has bought me for my birthday, and it's as I expected, not just unpleasant but brutally off-key. Although it was secreted, I found it during entirely everyday work around the house, believe me. This is a garment which might come under the heading of caftan, I believe. It's done in multitudinous foul colours and I would never go out in it for fear of guffaws, though I will have to wear it about the house on my birthday and maybe a day or two afterwards in order to give no offence to the malevolent, venomous swine. A list of the horrible colours follows: purple, magenta, light and dark green, ochre! Please pray for me having to don it, if you go to church around the time of my birthday. The theme of the caftan would appear to be harmony. I mean, enforced harmony, by shoving together tints that clash fiendishly and pretending they don't. He must have toured many shops doggedly before alighting on this creation.

Around the hearth in discursive mood, Dennis and I have been tirelessly trying to puzzle out the Iraq situation and its many complexities even now, especially the US dimension. Dennis believes the US and European influences will eventually come good, but, of course, some fish pastes have more brain than Dennis, and his devotion to the many films of Alain Delon imparts a Continental bias. Dennis is at the moment tirelessly engaged on a useless concordance of the principal and middling roles in all Alain Delon movies, and will shortly be visiting some London film library for detail, or that's the story. I would never deny he has energy, particularly if he's also doing something with Mrs AV Ward OBE and those thighs.

Many would say retaliate re. the birthday present and find him a gift equally scabby and wounding when it's his, or at Christmas. This I would regard as rather simplistic and negative, though – and infantile. My feeling is that, because he is so negligible, the best thing to get him is something negligible, never crudely and massively insulting. A full-out retaliation would dignify him, as if he were worth hurting. I shall probably look in hardware stores or the university bookshop.

An old school friend and her husband came to one of our weekend 'get-togethers' recently, and she seemed to enjoy herself considerably, and made an impression on a few other guests due to her suppleness etc, though her husband is a bit overly witty and that kind of thing. My suspicion is that of late she has been reduced to fantasy and private pleasuring and coming here really took her out of herself, as it were! She was impressed by a police officer who attends sometimes, very well built and so on, and originally from Aberdeen. He is known fondly as Scotland Yard. In his little way, Dennis is inclined to ask how I have this friend or that friend, as if my life only began when I met him, like I'm Eve, fashioned from a bit of Adam. Be assured, Mother, I give him wholly amicable and complete answers, because I know my time will eventually come. One day this topiary prince will learn there's more to life than privet.

I'm glad to say I feel considerably more relaxed because of his recent harmonious behaviour, yet always remaining alert, fear not, and I am writing this in the public library again, owing to the caftan reference. Stress has subsided, knowing he is occupied and, in his drab way, content. Some familiarity and even molestation from tramps and dossers who come into the library for a sit down are only inter-mittent in my experience. I will close wishing you, on behalf of Dennis and myself, all the very best.

Your loving daughter,
Jill

31

Carthage

Greg!
Friday's on. Possibly here. Yea, in this very property! He might go to London for some bollock-boring film research.

We'll dodge that hired Paul Pry in the Finesse somehow. I still think it would be wrong and too dangerous to take things further than evasion, though, at least to date. But, of course, I understand your feeling that something severe should be done about him.

My love, my love,
Jill

32

Carthage
Tabbett Drive
Exall DL2 4NG
7 July 2005

Dear Cindy

Just a formal note to say how much Dennis and I enjoyed seeing you and your husband in our home recently among our other dear guests. We both felt you 'lasted the pace' extremely well for a first visit and several friends have telephoned to speak appreciatively of 'the new acquisitions', meaning your good selves. Julian's wry humour in no way jarred, you can rest assured, especially as patently he has so many other facets to recommend him. Needless to say, you have facets also, and these were certainly appreciated, likewise. People could hardly believe you were a doctor, but I've often noticed that many members of your profession show a creditably unfussy attitude to their own and their spouse's health in the interests of exuberance, and, of course, as mentioned previously, you do know what remedies to apply in case of trouble.

If anything unexplainable ever happens to me, I would very much like you to get in touch as a matter of urgency with Mrs AV Ward OBE, who lives at the large house called Fairholm in the Drive. It's possible she would have information. I might leave something written and well-documented with her against eventualities, though I'm not altogether sure about this because she possibly has something juicy going with you know who. I don't want to draw you into anything. Approachable is a word that can certainly be used about her, but sometimes she wishes to be called Alice and sometimes Veronica. You will have to play it by ear.

Your thank-you card has just arrived and both Dennis and I think it is lovely, in the best traditional sense. We are jointly so sick of those which come with 'Recycled' written in green on both card and envelope so blatantly. Dennis remarked of a recycled Christmas card last year, 'Next it will have to be recycled turkeys, probably.' Quick for him and almost good enough for Julian! We also like the way you sign the card individually. That suggests both independence and harmony, we feel, which are equally so desirable, and our aim here. We greatly look forward to many more happy times together and we certainly hope you do, too.

Yours in true friendship,

Jill

33

Carthage
Tabbett Drive
Exall DL2 4NG
7 July 2005

Dear Tim,

I'm happy to say that the recent official beginning of summer cast a benign influence over our household, to such a degree that I wonder whether my troubles have finally ended – even wonder sometimes whether they were imaginary, though, of course, there is evidence to suggest the contrary.

You ask whether I have received any reply from Anna. Afraid not. It's possible, even likely, that I never shall. Perhaps the address I have is out of date. Perhaps she does not wish to be bothered with the distant troubles of someone who passed out of her life years ago, and in sad circumstances. That would be entirely understandable. She has made a new existence for herself, and I'm sure is perfectly content with her present man. It might activate old feelings, old pains, to put herself in touch with me again, or with either of us. Possibly it's best if we regard that fierce, rough-house chapter in our lives as over.

I've been in London for a couple of very enjoyable days, undertaking research on Alain Delon films, and I'm not at all sure what went on here in my absence. The point is, the people I reluctantly but unavoidably commissioned to handle surveillance seem to have botched things up. They are not dealing with fools. You know how it is, I expect, when someone has been in your home, unacknowledged to you? It is a sickening notion that an outsider should have been sitting secretly in this favourite chair or furtively handling books lovingly collected and cared for. It feels as if vandals had intruded. I'm not one to go sniffing for traces, I hope. That would be mean, indeed, despicable. It's simply a question of the build-up of affront and revulsion. These I suppress, if only on account of the happy weather. I assure you I shall do nothing precipitate. That's not my way now, believe me.

Your brother,
Dennis

34

Carthage
Tabbett Drive
Exall DL2 4NG
10 July 2005

My dear Mother,

I've just this moment returned from Veronica's (or Alice's, if you'd prefer!) where I was able to read, re-read and re-re-read your beautiful latest letter prior to routine disposal as per ritual. You're right, we are undoubtedly into summer now, and I have certainly mentioned to my friend, Cindy, not to talk unwisely anywhere about her times here, as we do not want all sorts wishing to take part; we are usually at capacity. Too many parked vehicles can become a desperate nuisance in Tabbett Drive. Dennis is *such* a great believer in consideration for the neighbours. Music is always kept low in volume etc, and while some cries of merriment, release, gratification and astonishment are probably inevitable, we do not encourage such showiness. Cindy, a doctor, and through-and-through qual-ified, is accustomed to confidentiality.

No, I have not had to wear the disgusting caftan yet. I shan't receive it until my actual birthday. Dennis is very endearingly strict and sentimental about all the time-blessed, lovely rituals of a birthday, such as the surprise of opening parcels in his actual presence on the day itself, so he can enjoy the reaction. I had to undo the string and wrapping paper to see the garment when I came across it inadvertently and I do hope I retied it properly because Dennis is the sort of man who is so sentimental about birthdays that he would be upset if he thought I knew what the gift was already and thus be deprived of a due surprise. He is the kind who would go out again, despite the heat, and exchange this present for something else so that I would be duly and fully surprised on my birthday morn. There are probably plenty of other hurtful presents he could think of. This would be upsetting for me because I have prepared myself for that caftan with certain ringing terms of thanks and wonderment at his brilliant choice. It is impera-tive to play him at his own swine-ish game.

The London research for his Delon concordance seems to have gone well. It really is an inspiration the way Denn enters so wholeheartedly into anything that interests him, such as films or the hedge creatures. This is a family trait on his side, with his father always pursuing an interest, such as reassemblies of old televisions. Interests are their long suit. He returned much refreshed after a comfortable journey despite holidaymakers and terrorism fear, with very good meals on both ways in the diner. Loneliness in his absence does not greatly perturb me as I am able to use the time for thinking about topics that tend to get neglected in the usual hurly-burly. Almost meditation! For instance, on the economic front, the signs are confusing, aren't they? Some say that house prices continue to sink, others that the market has begun to recover. And still trouble over the total, prov-able surrender of arms in Ireland. Everywhere in the world there are these weary moves towards peace, yet so many come to nothing. I thought of going to the library again to write this as he

Look, I'll close now. Certain pressures. But it really is all right. Don't grow anxious, PLEASE. How the time flies, though, doesn't it? Don't think I am sweeping the matter of your visit under the carpet, but it might be wiser overall if I came to you.

Yours,
Jill

35

TRANSCRIPT OF INTERVIEW BETWEEN COUNSEL-LOR ELAINE ROBERTS AND MRS JS, 18 JULY 2005

ER: First thing I'd like to ask, Jill, is whether you mind if I record our conversation. It's not usual in counselling, but not unknown, either. The advantage is, we can each have a copy to study at the end.

JS: OK.

ER: I've read the outline of your early life which you've kindly written for us, and the several other papers you brought in.

JS: You've looked at the letter he sent about Mr Nelmes, have you?

ER: What is it that makes you seek counselling?

JS: One of my neighbours was counselled recently and said it helped.

ER: Probably by a colleague here, Susan Wright.

JS: Yes, that could be it.

ER: We all have our own way of doing things, Jill. Myself, I like to look at least a little into a client's childhood.

JS: A lovely, joyous childhood.

ER: Yes, as you've described it on paper here. And you light up when you mention it. Your eyes shine.

JS: The memories shine, Elaine. Don't your own memories of childhood shine? To know one's place.

ER: To know one's place?

JS: Never that kind of certainty again.

ER: Father, mother, equally loving towards you, and loving towards each other?

JS: Oh, yes. Unstinting. You, by your training, I suppose, look for signs of things a-tilt. Nil. Tea and many other meals all together around the family table, walks, so full of talk and really well-meant promises. No smudgeon of abuse, so fashionable in recollection now. Absolutely nothing physical. Nothing I remember.

ER: And then two sisters?

JS: The same comforting relationship. Older. So good to me. Not soft. Decent sibling rivalry, of course. But tender. You, Elaine, do you have a brother or sister?

ER: Yet now you're not in touch?

JS: There was no abrupt break, no drift to coldness. My sisters and I went our own ways. That's adulthood. One of them sends a birthday card. My parents treated me as a person from a very young age. You knew your place and the family gave you a place. Do you know what I mean? They allowed me to be myself, in very large measure. Unconstrained.

ER: And you married quite young, I think?

JS: Are you saying I was looking for a replacement to continue such a harmonious home life? As it were, looking in a panic because I realized childhood was over, and finding Denn? That it was too hurried. An error.

ER: Is that how you see it, Jill?

JS: Never. A summer wedding. That was true joy stretching into more joy.

ER: What was it in Dennis that caught your attention?

JS: Elaine, I expect you are wondering whether that bit of letter about Mr Nelmes I brought in is genuine? Did I hatch it myself?

ER: Tell me what you thought you saw in Dennis originally.

JS: I want to bring him in here. If you saw him, talked to him for a while I think you'd understand.

ER: That would be ideal, Jill. And he'd come?

JS: Could you say, just like that, what drew you to *your* man, Elaine? Any of them? Are you married? No ring, and sometimes you look very hurt and sad. Something missing? It's the norm for us as women, yes? He's not averse to coming here. He has total respect for what you're doing – for what Communicate, the organization, is doing. Any organization with a full duke as its patron would impress Denn. If he came, you'd find him completely amenable. Being amenable is not Denn's long suit, but he does know how to be amenable sometimes.

ER: He knows you come, then?

JS: Obviously that letter extolling Nelmes had gone when I looked again on the computer, which I'm entirely entitled to do, it being joint-owned, though I make little use. That means he has finished it and sent it, then wiped the screen. Or he wants me to think he sent it. This would be for his own purposes. He's not short of those. Luckily, I'd taken a copy.

ER: Might he have had you followed here? Is that how he knows you're being counselled? Have you spoken to him?

JS: He runs his own life – trips to London, for creaky, unbelievable reasons. He had a letter from South Africa, cleverly using his initials on the envelope, not first name, but probably of some dirty intimacy, no business matter. Handwritten. Are you telling me South African firms haven't heard of typed address labels?

ER: Has there been any change in how you see Dennis now, compared with when you married?

JS: Always, I knew there were depths.

ER: That attracted you?

JS: Would *you* be attracted by depths in a man, Elaine?

ER: You wished to explore these depths, did you?

JS: Are you trained not to answer my questions, but always to turn them back? It doesn't seem fair. Like the third degree.

ER: You're the client. Does it bother you to be questioned? Why?

JS: As to his depths, in a humorous novel I read once a character says about another, 'Deep down he's shallow'.

ER: That's what you found in Dennis?

JS: Do you never have domestic troubles, Elaine – relationship troubles?

ER: Perhaps I'd get counselled by someone else if I did. *I'd* face the questions then. Did either of your parents ask you a lot of questions?

JS: I think you *do* have troubles. It's the way you look so broken sometimes.

ER: Does he know you found the letter to the investigation firm on the screen and noted later it had gone?

JS: Nothing has come that looks like a reply to it in, say, a properly typed business envelope marked 'Private and Confidential'. But they wouldn't write, people like that. Phone calls. Nothing on paper.

ER: The letter said he had reports. *They'd* be written, wouldn't they?

JS: Oh, reports. But mostly phone jobs – no record. Obviously, what you really want to say is that that letter he wrote and its phrasing – 'distasteful', 'unambiguous' etc – makes it sound like two people actually indulging sexually and monitored by this Nelmes. That's what you and your colleagues would conclude. This is obvious. And the bit about 'evidence for a court'.

ER: Is that how it was?

JS: Rebutting, I ask, why aren't there photographs? I thought gumshoes always did pictures as verification.

You can get cameras that work in the dark, on body heat. If this had happened there would be body heat, wouldn't there?

ER: People who come here are often very frank – frank and truthful. They're looking for solutions to a problem. They bring all the facts. Jill, they know the thing can't work otherwise. Are you bringing me all the facts? Or are some of the facts not facts?

JS: So what you're saying is I have this lovely childhood and then get into a marriage too fast with some jerk who can't think further than gangster movies and hedge clippings, and I'm driven like a thousand others to escapism, fantasy? Dream of having it off with someone else, dream of being peeped at. Dream of a husband, jealous to a gratifying point where he hires a detective. And these imaginings keep me going? Is that your thesis?

ER: Tell me what you meant by depths. 'You always knew he had depths,' you said. That's not just gangster films and topiary.

JS: Rest assured, I do see the relevance of these questions, Elaine. You've had your training – your line being, if you can determine what brought us together it might be possible to do some repair work.

ER: It's a start. I wonder why you're so suspicious of counselling's methods.

JS: Depths are depths. Look, it's as if now there are areas about himself he doesn't understand, so, obviously, I don't understand them either. You can feel a yearning in him to branch out, aspire, even though he's pulpy. That can be very exciting. Look, no mystery, this letter he had from South Africa will be from a woman called Anna, then Bates, known to me from years back and considerate yet ebullient in those days. I don't mean I've seen her letter. He made sure. But I know. She impinged markedly on the lives of both of them, Dennis and his brother, Tim. She has a really terrific brain by any standard, with a great deal of time for Dennis. And for his brother. Her partner/husband is a scientist of genuine mark over there, employed in a thriving industry. I'd imagine it's a big, Jo'burg, enclave house with lights, razor wire and dogs, in view of the crime rate. This is the scale of values we're talking about, you see. Well, I know it's Jo'burg, because I saw the address on the envelope flap.

ER: You resent that he's still in touch with her?

JS: What I meant by 'depths'. What you'd say is confront him on all these scores, I imagine.

ER: Have you thought of that?

JS: Or are you saying to yourself, I'll call this client's bluff?

ER: We have a way of working which has proved itself in the past, that's all. You reach a stage where head-on has to be an option, and possibly the best. Do you draw back from that?

JS: When I bring Dennis in here to the counselling room – well, I mean, that's not the way to put it, not at all. Dennis is hardly someone to be brought or taken by anyone. A dear, inventive man in so many ways and cooperative, but never domineered. When Dennis decides to come in you will see for yourself the 'depths'. Even you, Elaine, cool and precise. He can be contemplative himself, in his own way. And I see that as an asset, in some respects. Win his confidence and he'll probably offer to vivify your privet, yet this is only a minor gesture, like offering a cigarette in the old days. Rapport with Dennis can go far beyond that, and might well.

ER: Does he frighten you, Jill?

JS: I'm quite safe walking a very precise line, and who can say more? Can you? I come here for advice and I feel a bonding with you, Elaine. Yet I walk this line totally alone, obviously. Victoria Cross stuff?

36

My dearest Greg,

Please do be patient. The high-summer period is bound to be tricky, with all these damn neighbourly barbecues which I can't get out of, and which, of course, he attends. I'm sure it's the same for you. I think of you always during these chore parties with their presiding sirloins and imitation champers, believe me. Will be in touch the very soonest I can see free time for us.

BELIEVE IN ME, GREG.

Adoringly,
Jill

37

Carthage
Tabbett Drive
Exall DL2 4NG
20 July 2005

My dear mother,

Such a fine party at Mrs AV Ward's to celebrate her receipt

of the OBE, connected with her work in the Department of Employment or Police Authority or Probate Office, or one of those rubbish dumps. She was a Queen's Birthday Honour, and really she put on such a fuss you'd think the Queen lucky to have someone like Alice to award the OBE to.

I was able to present her officially with two very select blue cut-glass vases from Dennis and me, which he naturally thought marked the award of the medal, but Mrs AV Ward, OBE, and I knew that at least one vase was a further thank-you for her considerate services as a secure pigeon-hole for my mail. This was why I insisted on a pair. One might have been sufficient for the OBE, very ordinary as awards go. Not quite like being made a Dame.

I was delighted to hear you had written to thank the worthy old hunk for her help. The vases will stand at each end of Alice's mantlepiece, like minor monuments commemorating our triumph, yours and mine! I will be able to draw additional happiness from the sight of them as I sit reading your letters in private, temporarily wholly secure.

Mainly a barbecue for the celebration, but some inside activity, also. The food was first class, including smoked trout etc. At first she said she had thought it would be wrong to accept the award because it was her whole department which deserved recognition and she feared to look invidious, or something like that. Such a wholesome and characteristic reaction. She came round, though, and, as you'd expect, turned as invidious as hell. Dennis is certainly interested in her, perhaps already on board. I could smell it, yet she is a trifle married. When he is in her company I spot that diffidence and eye-shine which is Dennis's usual little way to signify hormones. Often I used to get the feeling when reading about the rather active activities of the younger members of the Royal Family, that it might help them if only they could come to one of our weekend gatherings and express themselves fully.

Meanwhile, things are anything but good with retail trade in this country because of high interest rates.

Dennis has his own slippery little thoughts at such a party

as Mrs AV Ward's and he would regard it as real kudos to get amongst an OBE, regardless of age and hips. It's not so much his shallowness that defeats me as his belief in his own uniqueness and grace as a human being.

Accordingly, I am writing this again in the public library reading room, where I think I previously mentioned Scrumpy-breathed tramps, in for a rest, may come and sit by you and try familiarity, poor deprived dears. If some of my writing gets a bit untoward you will know it's because I'm dealing with such an intrusion.

Well, as to intrusion, I feel I gave Dennis a lease on me – my entity, body etc – and it's run out. Nothing rupturous, just time-expired. It will seem unusual to be flushing pieces of your timely letters down a toilet bowl used routinely by a recipient of the Order of the British Empire. She's burly, especially low and would sit very heavily. I said nothing to Dennis following the OBE party about his tawdry, blood-up interest in her, which might only be a swoon at her probably merited gong. I wanted no recip-rocal snarling. If you recall a girl called Anna, also of some hip size, who took on both Dennis and his brother unstintingly, I think he might be exchanging ideas there again by air mail, she having married a foreigner where she was not known. As I recall it, some friend of hers went missing and I heard she never turned up anywhere. I will let you know if it's necessary to stop using Mrs AV Ward's address. Obviously she might suffer conscience difficul-ties were she sixty-nining with Dennis while still offering her letter box to me! (Sorry!)

It is now correct to address her as Mrs AV Ward, OBE, even though the actual conferring by Her Majesty in person at a Buckingham Palace garden party is some way off. This we shall hear rather a lot about. Oh, God! Women do find his shallowness winning, being unable to believe there can be so much of it, and wishing to plumb – how it happened to me, possibly. Also, there is vigour. He can look almost exotic and more or less unpoignant when on his little stepladder in sweatshirt and olive green summer trousers. It seemed satisfactory, also, during the OBE party, to think of him using that toilet bowl and gazing down affectionately on a run-of-the-mill, Valpol-aided stream etc, unaware of this bowl's further, richer role month in month out taking your letters out of his damn ambit.

Well, I will close now, wishing to see whether there are any further developments in the situation re the Northern Ireland problem. Dennis, I know, would wish to be remembered to you most warmly and has asked me to remind you to be alert to sudden changes in the summer weather.

Your loving daughter,
Jill

38

Carthage

My dearest Greg,

Picking through his creepy things very systematically over a space of an hour plus, when he inadvertently left his filing cabinet keys behind yesterday, I happened to come across certain documents which I have photocopied at the public library and which I am sending you now. I will be marking the big envelope 'Private and Confidential', which I certainly hope is observed in view of meaningful contents! I naturally made copies for myself, also, though I do not know whether it will be wise for me to keep them owing to his trawling tendencies. I may dispose of them in the toilet of a friend who has been awarded the OBE, and which I know will dispose of them fully over a period of several days to avoid clogging, as long as given possibly two flushes each time – even this bulk when torn small. I could not risk having any fraction of them left behind and floating in our own toilet and we have no open fires. Don't worry, I have replaced the originals in his filing cabinet exactly as found and he will never suspect. They were in a file marked 'Activities', just like that, as if they were about rock climbing or lacrosse! Well, you'll see I've written some comments here and there in the margin, these reports made me so triumphant or sick or angry or sad, mostly angry. Very.

Of course, the other thing is he could have left the keys around purposely in his creepy way, but I looked very carefully for any wool strand or hair he might have fixed across the file-cabinet drawer to indicate illicit opening, and found nothing. Darling, we will obviously have to discuss this matter face-to-face as soon as we can, but these papers can change nothing, can they? Always remember that. Nothing.

You'll notice I've scissored out one or two sections of the report. These contained a total misreading by Mr JJP Nelmes of events in the reference room of the public library. He has a base mind, perhaps essential in his kind of dirty work. Who heard of people with three initials doing such a miserable, even evil, job? When his parents took the long trouble to think up three names it was because they expected him to turn out to be brilliant and wholesome, such as a great rugby player or an historian, not a prat who swallows sickening gossip from prurient staff in a public library. Despite my temperate words in the past, I now find it a towering offence that someone of D's sort should remain in decent health while retaining such material as below. But I do like some of the descriptive stuff! Believe me, it is nothing but gratifying that your mouth was open so wide in expressions of pleasure that Nelmesy could note your back fillings (see his account of things). His last report is truly beautiful – and there we were, comfy inside and at one, while he fretted.

Yours for ever,
Jill

39

Nature of document: Clandestine surveillance of Mrs Jill Seagrave

Time: Various periods as specified by client

Signatory of document: JJP Nelmes

Distribution of document: Client
Office Principal
Copy retained by signatory
STRICTLY NO OTHERS

Serial number of document: 1

Date of Job: 10 June 2005

Time: Begins 17.30

Conditions (light/dark): l

Photographs: Nil

Description:

I observed the subject leave her home alone at 17.50 in a Toyota saloon, and followed by car. She was obviously pre-occupied by thoughts of the immediate future and remained unaware of my presence. At 18.10 she arrived at The Downs district of Exall and took the road towards Masterton Woods. I observed a white Volvo waiting near the edge of the woods, unlit. A man was alone in the car, at the wheel. Subject drove alongside the Volvo and stopped. This is a road little used in the evenings and to avoid attention I drove on for some distance and returned on foot. By the time I reached the cars, subject was in the back of the Volvo with the man.

Can't deny it, can we Greg?

The engine of the Volvo was running, presumably to produce warm air for the heater, the evening having grown chilly. I approached with care and took up a crouched position close to the nearside rear door window. From this spot I could observe both parties were unclothed at least to the waist, my lower vision being at this stage limited. Each held in one hand what appeared to be a partially eaten fruit turnover, or possible meat pasty, and with the other hand fondled each other, then fiercely embraced.

Fiercely is so right. It happens so rarely, love.

Occasionally, during pauses, one of the two would pick up from the floor of the car a claret bottle and each would take long drinks from it, passing it one to the other, generally this transference accompanied by a kiss.

Not just generally. Every lovely damn time.

After some minutes, the two disappeared below window level, except for the occasional glimpse of the naked rear quarters of a man. Also, from time to time, a pair of feet and legs would appear above window level and may have touched the ceiling of the Volvo. The feet/legs were far apart. Unquestionably, an act of coition was taking place.

No, really! Greg, does he know any woman who can do it with her legs together?

There were in due course cries of pleasure, both male and female, audible above the sound of the running engine. While they were preoccupied, I was able to stand up for a clearer view and confirm the above. Both parties were entirely unclothed now, the garments being piled in disorderly fashion on the front seats, as if the parties had disrobed very hurriedly without regard for creasing or tidiness. The wine bottle had been placed on the rear window ledge, also two further uneaten fruit turnovers or pasties. The engine was still running, but above it I could hear the occasional pleasured groans and some words. These included 'darling' reiterated four times at volume by the subject and 'take', also repeated several times by the subject, this at almost scream level.

Even reading the account by this plonker gets my heart speeding, Greg.

The man also spoke the word 'darling' once, and mentioned in loving tones the subject's hair using the rare term 'aureate'. His accent appeared to be Scottish, educated.

I had approached the vehicle from the near or feet/legs/hindquarters side, suitable for ascertaining behaviour but not helpful in definite identification. I therefore moved around seeking sight of the man's face. This was successful because, during the sexual exertions, his face came at times very close to the rear-side window or pressed against it and I was able to note, in fading daylight, the following:

Age: 35–40 years old
Race: Caucasian
Colouring: fair/brown hair; light skin; eyes possibly blue
Moustache: No

Beard: No
Description: Long, thin face. Long straight nose. Wide, heavy-lipped mouth. No apparent balding. Small, even teeth, seemingly all present, many at the back heavily filled. Despite some distortion of the features, due to the exigencies of the circumstances – leading to occasional sudden thrusting of his face against the window – the features appeared to be of some sensitivity.

Only some you unobservant sod, Nelmesy?

Possibly a professional rather than of artisan class. This impression was also given by his right hand likewise pressed now and then against the window as if for extra leverage, and which appeared long-fingered, fine and well cared for. The contact of the man's face and hair against the window created clear patches on the steamed glass, facilitating observation.

Resting, in due course, the two sat up, remaining in the rear seat and very close with occasional kissing. They ate the remaining food and appeared to finish the opened bottle of claret. The man then produced another from the floor and, leaning over the front seat, found a corkscrew in the pocket of his discarded navy blazer. He opened the bottle and they began to drink from this one, as before. They spoke, but now in tones too low for me to hear above the sound of the engine, which continued to run. They laughed a great deal and mock-fought, taking sudden bites from each other's turnover/pasty, as if stealing portions, or like seagulls disputing items on a rubbish tip.

What's that bloody poem you go on about sometimes, Greg, with amorous birds of prey tearing away at each other? Did JJP Nelmes do the same literature correspondence course as you?

I became aware suddenly from the way they glanced about and seemed to grow restless that they intended to come out of the car, regardless of light rain which was falling, and of being naked. I withdrew hurriedly to the cover of a copse, from which I could still observe. The man now switched off the engine and they left the car. Outside, they held each other and began to dance in a slow, grave style, both humming and sometimes singing the well-known old tune 'Every Time You Say Goodbye'.

Slow, grave, sad style. Still an unobservant bastard. Of course sad. Goodbyes all the time.

The man still held a claret bottle and occasionally they drank from it, while continuing to dance. I observed him to be about six feet tall and slimly built – about 168 pounds or less. They spoke occasionally but I was too far off to hear all they said.

Thank God.

The following are words I recollected and wrote up immediately it was convenient. They are not an exhaustive or continuous sequence, owing to inaudible matter intervening:

Man: It's like that scene in *Lady Chatterley's Lover*.
Subject: Always some book has done it first.
Subject: Do I feel him stirring again?
Man: He's shower proof.
Subject: One hundred per cent proof.
Man: But only a small stepladder?
Subject: No useful altitude at all, but the automated shears could be useful.

Christ!

Subject: I wish we could be seen now.
Man: Who by?
Subject: Anyone.
Man: We wouldn't want to be seen drinking Ducru-
             Beaucaillou 1987 from the bottle, for God's
             sake. Villainous.
Subject: I adore its grape-based grapey grapiness.
Man: Ah, you've been reading the experts.

At 20.20 the couple returned to the rear seat of the Volvo. In due course, I believe love-making took place again. Witnessing one act being sufficient for court requirements, I did not move into a close position again, this being liable to involve further, now unnecessary, risk, and constituting gratuitous prying.

Such delicacy.

However, if the client wishes for exhaustive observation, I shall in future seek to document fully all intimate incidents. It appeared that the subject was this time in the top position, the soles of her feet occasionally being pressed against the side window, smaller than male feet, and in any case recognizable from the previous observation, the central toe of the left foot being notably crooked, as if from wearing unsuitable shoes as a child. Her feet during this second incident were, of course, now reversed (since she was positioned on top) and mud coated. At 21.15 the couple quickly dressed and the man cleaned the window with a rag. He left the car briefly and put two bottles into the bushes. The two kissed and the subject returned to her own car. They drove away. I recovered the two bottles, labelled Château Ducru-Beaucaillou, Saint-Julien, Médoc 1987, with a picture of a large stone building at its centre. Because my car was at a distance, I could not follow either vehicle but drove to the subject's home and found the Toyota parked there. The time was 23.20. I remained in position until 00.01, as agreed with client, but the subject did not re-emerge.

Indications:

1. The man would appear to be healthy and of some literary knowledge, possibly with a taste for old Ella Fitzgerald numbers and, in view of dancing in the rain, possibly also playful and/or unconventional, even theatrical.

   'Romeo, Romeo, wherefore art thou, Romeo?'

2. If he, and not the subject, brought the bottles, he may be an *amateur du vin*, since, on inquiry, I find this to be a very reputable claret and he was ashamed of drinking it from the bottle. Such expertise might indicate a high salary or standard of living.
3. I was unable to study his clothes at any length, because, for most of the period of observation, they were heaped casually on the front seat, but the double-breasted navy blazer with silver buttons looked to be of distinguished cut, when he went to dispose of the bottles, and his fashion boots were leather.

Matters arising:

1. Ask client if he can identify the man from: a) Car make and/or registration, which I can of course provide. b) Physical description. c) Possible Scottish accent. d) Probable social/educational classification. e) Other factors.
2. Check with client whether the wine is from *his* cellar, having been brought by subject, not man.
3. Make confidential inquiries to trace vehicle registration if 1. fails. Discuss possible expensive hire of special

camera for possible night work, especially as the days grow shorter.

JJP Nelmes

*

Nature of document:	Clandestine surveillance of Mrs Jill Seagrave
Time:	Hours specified by client
Signatory of document:	JJP Nelmes
Distribution of document:	Client Office Principal Copy retained by signatory STRICTLY NO OTHERS
Serial number of document:	2
Date of job:	15 June 2005
Time:	Begins 19.30
Conditions (light/dark):	l changing to d
Photographs:	Nil

Description:

I took up position near the subject's house at 19.30, as agreed with client, and she left in the Toyota at 20.08. I followed. She again appeared unaware of me. She drove to Duke Road in the Batten district of Exall, parked and walked from there to Constance Street where at 20.35 she went to number 23. I had also parked and kept close behind her, walking. At 23 she knocked on the door and was quickly admitted by the man I could identify by the hall light as the one from the previous meeting (Document 1) and whom we now know to be GRP of the home and business addresses specified to the client by telephone.

She remained in the house until 23.20, when she returned to her car and drove home. I followed and waited but she did not re-emerge.

I have no means of knowing what took place in the house between 20.35 and 23.20.

But I imagine he could make a guess, Greg!

Lights burned downstairs at number 23 when she arrived and a light was switched on upstairs at 20.55 and remained on until she left. Curtains were drawn both downstairs and upstairs. While waiting, I had walked around the area of Constance Street, Duke Road and Mortimer Road and observed the white Volvo parked in Mortimer Road.

Inquiries established that number 23 Constance Street is owned by Mr Neville D Haspen, a business colleague of GRP. Mr Haspen is divorced and is at present in Maryland, USA, on a sales trip.

Indications:

GRP, who has now been identified, has the use of 23 Constance Street while his colleague is abroad.

Matters Arising:

None new.

JJP Nelmes
*

Nature of document: Clandestine surveillance of
Mrs Jill Seagrave

Time:	Hours specified by client
Signatory of document:	JJP Nelmes

Distribution of document:	Client
	Office Principal
	Copy retained by signatory
	STRICTLY NO OTHERS

Serial number of document: 3

Date of job: 3 July 2005

Conditions (light/dark): l

Photographs: Nil

Description:

I took up position outside subject's home at 19.30. At 19.45 she left in the Toyota and drove towards the town centre. I followed. There she at once began tactics designed to escape surveillance, accelerating dangerously to overtake and put other vehicles between her and me, jumping traffic lights and using rapid turns into and out of side streets to confuse. I lost subject.

Right, right, right!

After searching the area for an hour I returned to the subject's home and found her Toyota parked there. I took up position and observed. There were lights on in several parts of the house, upstairs and down. At 00.01, when I ended my observation, nobody had left the house and all lights there were out.

Indications:

1. Subject knows she is under surveillance.

Give the man a coconut!

2. Her behaviour suggests she intended some clandestine activity at her home, client being absent.

Give him another coconut!

3. A person could have been picked up and taken to the house by her, or could have entered the house by arrangement and unobserved while I was following her/trying to find her.

And yet another!

Matters arising:

1. It is essential to change surveillance vehicle.
2. It might also be necessary to change operative (self) following apparent recognition.
3. I will suspend surveillance pending client's instructions.

JJP Nelmes

40

Well, I bumped into Jill and Dennis in the street and, really, I picked up nothing to suggest they might be thinking of a move. Certainly there is still no For Sale board on the house. Dennis talks with all the usual enthusiasm of new hedge creatures he is considering for Carthage – a bison has taken his fancy, I gather, after seeing some in a Western film, and a cormorant – and I cannot believe he would be contemplating that kind of effort if they meant to go. A bison and a cormorant are really quite distinctive and complex creatures when done in leaves – the bison's horns, the cormorant's extended neck – and it would seem almost irresponsible to scheme such works were one intending to abandon them. In any case, if the house is put up for sale now with the present peacock, hares and seagull represented in the hedges, a buyer might feel irritated when upon purchase he discovered the outside decoration had been altered.

Perhaps, though, my wish is father to the thought. I do not want them to go and I am possibly eager to see signs that they mean to remain. Somehow they have for me become integral to Tabbett Drive, part of its character, if this is not too fancy a thought. The place would be substantially changed and probably diminished should they leave. In my perhaps slightly melodramatic but nonetheless genuine way I do believe there are people who can confer a vivid personality upon some otherwise routine locale. They seemed very relaxed together, no evidence of that restlessness which sometimes does afflict Jill. They behaved like a couple delighted with each other's company and with their present situation. How do *they do it, one may ask, while feeling grateful that they do, because one can, oneself, derive comfort and strength from them.*

41

TRANSCRIPT OF SECOND INTERVIEW BETWEEN COUNSELLOR ELAINE ROBERTS AND MRS JS, 25 JULY 2005

ER: The joy that lights up for your face and eyes, Jill, when I mention your childhood . . .

JS: Oh, yes, yes.

ER: There it is again! Really a tonic.

JS: For me as well, Elaine.

ER: What I'd like us to do is look a little deeper for its causes. Perhaps we need to know what your childhood provided, and then ask whether that's missing from your marriage. The mystery ingredient! We may find something for you and your husband to work on.

JS: So, you can see some positives, Elaine? This sounds really heart-warmingly constructive.

ER: Well, I hope we're always that.

JS: And I really am grateful.

ER: Our job. You said your parents encouraged you from when you were quite young to develop as a person, to be yourself.

JS: Oh, yes, yes.

ER: How did they do that?

JS: They have this wondrous, intense relationship, warm, coarse, witty, competitive, tender, yet I never felt excluded. Encompassed – I was gloriously encompassed.

ER: And your sisters?

JS: Yes, but I above all – they'd admit this, my sisters, I think – I above all was brought in, enveloped. Yes, brought in, that's the phrase.

ER: How?

JS: You mean you don't believe it?

ER: Jill, why do you think I might not believe it?

JS: Look, when I say brought in I don't mean anything suspect or physically dubious.

ER: Did you believe I'd think it was something suspect or physically dubious?

JS: Parents can have a good and full relationship with a child, girl or boy, and there still be nothing suspect or physically dubious.

ER: You feel that should be stated, do you, Jill? What would you say 'brought in' did mean, then?

JS: You're thinking about that father–daughter stuff in *Tender Is The Night*, I suppose. No. Not at all. But my parents might be having some conversation – politics, boxing, books, crime, wine – and they would turn and encompass me, want my view. My mother, tall, her hair worn bobbed, always bobbed – that was how she saw herself in those days – and my father, his brow unlined, no matter how heavy the subject we were discussing, and his vocab, well just his own – words like 'plangent' and 'uncensorious'.

ER: This is graphic, Jill.

JS: Are you saying you don't believe it – that it's just wordage and fantasy?

ER: Why do you ask that, I wonder. But is this all you mean when you say 'brought in'? They invited you into their conversations? Is that the extent of what you're saying?

JS: What else? Listen now, Elaine, none of this involved the least physical contact. This was all at the level of discussion, things on a pleasant – no it was more than pleasant, much more – bracing level of mental contact. I profited, unquestionably. It gave me range.

ER: Didn't you want physical contact?

JS: Not that they were in the least cold. I don't think my father knew how to frown in those days!

ER: How did they show their affection, then?

JS: Oh, I know some physical contact between parents and a child is lovely, and inevitable. Obviously, lifting and carrying when small. Some hugging. I see absolutely nothing untoward about that, the hands and so on entirely neutral.

ER: Would they hug you?

JS: Some children could be said positively to crave physical contact.

ER: Did you, Jill?

JS: Jill, you'll very soon be fully a woman, they might say, so admiringly. Almost singing the words, really.

ER: When would they say that? What would be happening? Which of them would say it?

JS: Oh, this would be during discussions. And they'd be thrilled to see how interested I was in grown-up topics, and how I could discuss them ably. My friends would be really surprised when I told them of what happened between me and my parents.

ER: What did happen?

JS: Haven't I told you? These talks and discussions with them at a well-informed level. Elaine, could I mention something?

ER: Well, of course. That's why we're here.

JS: All right. It's this: now and then I feel you think I'm speaking code – as if I might be saying things, but not saying them, hinting.

ER: Why do you believe I might think that?

JS: I use a word like joy about my childhood and it's clear you think, 'What's this overheated, pulpit vocabulary? What's dark underneath? What's this woman suppressing? What's she trying not to say to me, but trying to say to me? Is what happened in Jill's childhood a clue to what's happening now?' That's your

ER: training, Elaine. I certainly don't blame you for it.

ER: And *is* there something underneath. *Is* it code? Do you feel there might be factors from your childhood that would explain the present?

JS: A few of my friends had similar childhood experiences, so they were not as surprised as the others.

ER: Do you ever feel anger with your parents now about anything that happened in your childhood?

JS: I'd never talk to Dennis about those times.

ER: Do you ever feel anger with your parents now about anything that happened in your childhood?

JS: I've never seen Dennis show real anger himself. I know when he's displeased, obviously – that dear, has-been face suddenly skew-whiffed and ponderous. I know when he's evil. He has unparalleled control though, and I believe totally that it will continue like that, making matters endurable, at present, most probably.

ER: What is there for him to show anger *about*?

JS: If I told him of my childhood. In detail, clearly.

ER: Why should that anger him?

JS: He'd feel excluded – *not* encompassed. He thrives on envy, on imagining himself deprived. You see, my childhood's outside Denn's tiny, piss-arseing area. He has family, notably a brother but something a bit frightening in the relationship.

ER: Does he like you to have a life of your own?

JS: Well, I *am* still alive, Elaine.

ER: Do you regard yourself as inside his tiny area sharing it with him?

JS: Increasingly, I feel I will be able to manage Dennis, deal with Denn. Not to hurt your feelings, but I don't think it's much to do with counselling. Just, I see his structure in full now, such as it is. These days I can spot what makes him tick, not just what makes him a tick.

ER: *You* feel angry with *him*?

JS: Angry, angry. You like anger, do you? You regard anger as a plus. Do all counsellors like anger? They see it as another word for self-assertion. Myself, I think anger is mostly fear. And anger *is* one of the seven deadlies.

ER: You feel angry with him?

JS: Anger? I listen to him padding about on the fitted carpets. Well, it's his domain, so he's undoubtedly entitled. What's to say to him after these carpets have been fitted at quite a cost. He's worked for this house and the carpets. Beige mostly. And I watch him sussing out latent shapes in the privet. I don't know about angry exactly.

ER: Don't you feel anger that he believes you unfaithful and engages people to spy?

JS: This is what I mean, his 'tiny area'. Everything outside his little domain is terrifying to him, a hostile mystery, the poor, struggling dear, which, obviously, is what makes him so dangerous. In fact, you could say that in some ways he's beautifully brave even to look outside. In his own stunted terms, that is.

ER: So, you're outside, are you, Jill?

JS: You believe I'm spreading myself, then?'

ER: I wonder why you say that.

JS: 'Tiny area', yes, but in that 'tiny area', there are some good and lovely things, too, Elaine. That's why I'm here now, I suppose. I want to know how to make the best of those bits of normality and even goodness in him. But, look, I suppose our time's up.

ER: Ah, you're glad – relieved? I'm thinking about that word 'encompassed' you see. The word you used to cover relations with your parents. It doesn't sound like someone given freedom, does it?

JS: I wanted it.

ER: 'Encompassed' – isn't that more to do with being swallowed up, fenced in for a purpose, Jill? I wonder if that's really what you still want and are disappointed that Dennis is not strong enough to give it.

86

42

Carthage
Tabbett Drive
Exall DL2 4NG
30 July 2005

My dear Anna,

Oh, you do write such an amusing letter, even when the situation there at home must be so damnably tense for you! Amusing and brave: it is your humour and bravery along with other lovely attributes that I recall so vividly from that earlier time, of course. Were you to return, even under such circumstances, I know we would have many a laugh together, as well as comforting talks, obviously.

Incidentally, I trust you don't mind my letters being done on the word processor? I've almost forgotten how to hand-write! My feeling is that letters can still be wholly personal, despite being produced in this fashion, because it is still, after all, one mind speaking to another, with the machine a mere conduit, as a telephone might be.

The way you describe meals with him is funny and yet, of course, agonizingly painful and sad. 'Kindly pass the cruet, would you please?' One can almost feel the aggressive chill, especially when spoken with an Afrikaner accent, as I assume this would be. Your reports on what passes there have a real, wry lifelike quality. Have you ever thought of writing something – short stories or a novel? If you should return, I would have to insist, though, that Tim and his appallingly violent, ungovernable side is kept right out of things this time. His obsession with trying to stay young makes him despise wisdom, moderation and carefulness, because he deems these elderly characteristics. To which I reply, life is a learning experience and, the more experience one has, the more one is likely to make the right choices.

As you so perceptively say, the warmth of summer – even a Brit summer! – does, year-in, year-out bring a kind of solace. I, personally, would never regard the notion of seasonal optimism and so on as simply an empty stock-response brought on by the calendar, Anna. It has an enduring, pervasive, inspiring reality, and I feel I must get my behaviour in pleasant accord with the weather, even when matters here are basically amiss. Jill and I both love to sit in the evenings, perhaps outdoors on our garden furniture, gazing at the stars and moon, if there is one. I'm sure that, even in the strained circumstances of your present existence, you and Jan can also find some comfort in a favourable climate. I have to say, though, Anna, I would probably prefer it if this kind of intimacy between you and him did not persist! Well, not just probably – *definitely*. It's exciting to think you might be back in Britain so soon, even though, as I've said, the circumstances, admittedly, are unfortunate.

Without being petty, I hope, may I recount an incident that will illustrate the state of things between Jill and me? To my mind, it flies right against the whole lovely ethos of a birthday occasion (hers), darkening it unbelievably, and calling so much into question. For Jill's main present this year – there will be other, minor ones, naturally, so that I may witness more than once the enjoyable surprise element as she opens them (Anna, I do love to watch her excitement) – I had bought her a very attractive caftan. My conviction is that these garments are comfy to wear, often very becoming, multi-purpose and never out of date thanks to an exotic touch. For such a perfect gift, expense seemed a secondary matter. Bold in colouring, yet not at all garish, it had been cut with real style in silk. You cannot conceive, Anna, my sense of triumph in having found something so suitable after an arduous yet very worthwhile search.

Imagine, then, my astonishment when, on going through one of my personal drawers, where I keep a few private things including birthday presents ahead of the day, I realized that the gift, already charmingly wrapped by the shop, had disappeared. Yes, Anna, gone! At first, scarcely bothered, I thought I must have forgotten where I'd secreted it and looked in several other possible hidey-holes. Still no sign. Inevitably, I had to conclude finally that this article had been removed by Jill. I need not point out to someone as intelligent as you, Anna, that there are two extremely unpleasant implications. One: the lesser, yet disturbing just the same, is that Jill has no scruples about intruding insidiously upon small areas of our home which I deemed dedicated to me and inviolate. This conjures up an offensive picture. Two: that she would filch the gift for her own unspoken purposes.

I think I can reasonably claim to be a charitable person and I told myself that curiosity overwhelmed her, and she simply felt compelled to see what I had bought – as children will search for presents hidden away for Christmas. Accordingly, I waited for the gift to be returned secretly, rewrapped. I would certainly have said nothing, even if I'd noticed the wrapping was not exactly as before. There would have been something forgivable, even delightful, about such uncontrolled impatience in Jill.

However, the parcel has not been replaced to date (it being only a couple of days now to her birthday), and I can no longer believe it will be. Thus, I am compelled to believe, Anna, that, having taken the parcel and opened it, she was so captivated by the gift that she could not resist wearing the caftan to one or more of the personal things she slips out to in the evenings now and then or oftener. Probably, she realized too late that she could not refold and wrap it so both would look as new when, on her birthday eve, I came to fetch the parcel ready for the morn. Or, is it possible the caftan was damaged when worn on one of these special excursions? I have certain reasons, which I'll not go into now, for believing this could well happen to her clothing.

Again, had she but told me that her curiosity had got the better of her and that, subsequently, her thrilled approval of the garment made her determined to wear it as soon as possible, I do honestly believe I could have understood – could even have been gratified at the obvious, radiant success of the present. But silence.

Clearly, Anna, what is so hurtful, indeed, incomprehensible, is that she knew I was bound to come for the present on her birthday eve and would be utterly mystified and crestfallen at its absence. Is callous too strong a word for such behaviour? I fear not, Anna, and I venture to think you'd agree. Fortunately, though, I discovered the absence of the gift some while ago and, having waited and grown more and more sure it would not be returned, was able to go to the same shop and acquire a replacement caftan in, I'm pretty confident, the identical style, material and colours, and just as festively wrapped. My hunch that the original would never be returned proved dismayingly correct – or has done so, at least, until this late point. I have kept the second caftan in the locked boot of my car, and shall do until the very last moment, believe me!

Nothing will be said – not by me, that is – about the missing parcel, the expense being of no matter, although doubled, and I shall place this new gift on the table for breakfast opening as if this were the only one, and the one bought originally. I shall certainly keep all anger out of what I write on the gift tag.

No doubt all this will confuse Jill greatly, devastate her even, but I hope you will see I cannot be overly concerned about this when she has so obviously shut her eyes to the consequences of her behaviour upon me, and especially since it occurred at this supposedly celebratory time of the year. No doubt for my own birthday later she will buy some brilliantly inappropriate and possibly dangerous gift (or gifts, since she has much ingenuity, malice and determination) but, Anna, I would never dream of sneaking about in her own personal sections of our house so as to get 'early warning'. I will do as I always do, and what I deem to be required by a recipient of presents, which is to exclaim with humble joy not merely for the gifts themselves, but for the fine wrapping and bows.

Perhaps I have gone on a little about this caftan. Forgive me, if so. It is merely to illustrate, Anna, what things are like here. I don't think it's self-pitying or harsh to describe them in the term 'what I have to contend with'. But you must write and let me know how things are going for you as soon as you can.

With great affection,
Yours,
Dennis

43

Carthage
Tabbet Drive
Exall DL2 4NG
30 July 2005

Dear Tim,

No, regrettably, I still hear nothing from Anna and, in fact, the last letter I sent has been returned by the Post Office with the words 'Gone Away', so that's that. As I said earlier, perhaps on the whole, it is for the best, Tim. All three of us are, after all, married now, and all three of us are probably very different people from who we were in those troublesome, fascinating, savage days. They are times that cannot be recreated, and I am not sure I would

91

want them recreated, even if it were possible. I'm never quite convinced that Anna really approved of the way we settled those difficulties – how we were compelled to settle them. I can still see we had no alternative.

Naturally, Jill spotted the returned South African mail arrive, and also observes the envelopes from you, and is full of interest, though she never says anything. She would, of course, steam them open if I happened to be out or away when they came, so we must pray this does not happen. For herself, she has her own sly little way of receiving mail. Luckily, though, I have been able to form a nice friendship with her personal 'post mistress' a few houses away, so I might be able to persuade her towards disclosure eventually. In many ways, she's a sweet thing, though a little old and rather tense, as if scared. My London arrangement is, I think, on its last legs – recriminations despite gifts, and doubts and aggro – so don't imagine I'm madly seeking love in all directions, though, by God, the way Jill regards me, that would be quite understandable. To her I'm Alain Delon's pictures and the hedge creatures, and that's it – 'Dennis Seagrave, This is Your Measly Little Life!'

Of course, on the basis of reports, one already has enough to bring our marriage to an end. But I am not sure I want that yet. Believe me, this has nothing to do with her own and/or her parents' money. Simply, I want to find out the full story, Tim, in my old, obsessively thorough way. Plus, I still harbour some of those original feelings for Jill, and they grow especially significant around her birthday and other anniversaries. Apart from that, the whole prospect of divorce – the long drawn-out procedures, the complexities – fills me with apprehension and I find myself wondering whether there is not a quicker, more head-on means of dealing with this. You know your brother – not brilliant or even bright, but able on occasions to get right through to the essential facts – this despite warnings from the past. Oh, you'll think me very inconsistent, I expect!

Without being petty, I hope, may I recount an incident to illustrate the state of things between Jill and me? To my mind . . .

Perhaps I have 'gone on' a little about this caftan. Forgive me, if so. It is merely to illustrate, Tim, what things are like here. I don't think it's self-pitying or harsh to describe them in the term 'what I have to contend with'. But you must write and let me know how things are going for you as soon as you can.

Incidentally, I trust you don't mind my letters being done on the word processor? I've almost forgotten how to hand-write! My feeling is that letters can still be wholly personal when produced in this fashion, because it is still, after all, one mind speaking to another, with the machine a mere conduit, as a telephone might be . . .

With great affection,
Yours,
Dennis

44

Carthage

Dear Greg,

I feel a great need to be in touch with you today, as my birthday approaches. Perhaps we'll be able to enjoy this day together in the future, but meantime writing this will have to do! Plus, of course, I'll be consoling myself with the knowledge that your, so far, mysterious gift will turn out to be wonderful, and I'm sure the card is sexy. Mr Bush is certainly getting some stick over Iraq. It's a pity that the way his eyes are makes him look so nervy.

I expect we'll be visiting some bistro he's fond of for my birthday dinner, and I'll be thinking of you throughout, count on it. He's been very busy lately, churning out things on the word processor in his lair – probably printing off the same stuff over and over for his letters, with just the names computer-adjusted. That would be *so* like him. Economical. The copying and churning out is easy with a processor, as you know. I believe there are still fine things to Dennis, for instance his comparative cleanliness and care not to 'get people's backs up' with too much hedge-cutting talk, but he remains gravely problematical.

The sod has been working a typically brutal birthday ploy against me. I don't know if I told you but he had bought a totally vile caftan, which he had hidden away for my birthday morn. I happened to find this and was luckily able – after quite a deal of hesitation – to drop it, and the wrapping paper, into a builder's skip in the next road. Well, all credit to the scheming, persistent lout, when he discovered what had happened he went out and bought another, exactly the filthy same. I should really have been able to foresee that, knowing him so well.

It was wonderful that we could both break out for a little while the other evening, despite our eternal spy! I'm writing this in the public library, because it's safer like that. I feel more secure among people.

Till soon, love,
Jill

45

Carthage
Tabbett Drive
Exall DL2 4NG

My dear Marie,

I felt a great need to write and thank you for the lovely time we had together in London on my 'Alain Delon' expedition a little while ago. I'm really writing because of something you said during that visit. You did not seem prepared to believe the relationship here was as bad as I described, and you appeared to be suggesting I was 'using' you. I rebutted that then, and wish to do so again – and again and again.

Incidentally, I trust you don't mind my letters being done on the word processor? I've almost forgotten how to handwrite! My feeling is that letters can still be wholly personal when produced in this fashion, because it is still, after all, one mind speaking to another, with the machine a mere conduit, as a telephone might be.

Without being petty, I hope, may I recount an incident that will illustrate the state of things between Jill and me? To my mind . . .

Perhaps I have 'gone on' a little about this caftan. Forgive me, if so. It is merely to illustrate, Marie, what things are like here. I don't think it's self-pitying or harsh to describe them in the term 'what I have to contend with'. But you must write and let me know how things are going for you as soon as you can.

D

46

GREG
   THAT'S YOUR NAME, YES?
   YOU KNOW I'VE GOT YOUR NUMBER, MATEY.

47

Carthage
Tabbett Drive
Exall DL2 4NG
1 August 2005

Dear Mr Lavery,
   I am enclosing a further cheque in final payment for your services. I still regard Mr Nelmes' work as of high quality and it was simply very unfortunate that somehow he was identified, and surveillance was then suspended, as you know. I don't think I would wish to have my concerns taken over by another of your firm's operatives – admirable as I am sure they all are – so I will not trouble you to follow that recommendation in Mr Nelmes' last report. In any case, as

has already been suggested by Mr Nelmes, we are not really in need of any further information, and I feel that, in my admittedly amateur fashion, I can personally handle any small problems of evidence which might present themselves henceforward.

Yours sincerely,
DW Seagrave

48

1 August 2005

Dear Peregrine,

Dear one, please, please, you MUST NOT come to this house ever again. The library is our spot, and thereabouts naturally – giving that creepy gumshoe the slip! I don't know how you found my address. I'm sure I never mentioned it, not that I want to be secretive, obviously. I am going to bring this by hand to the reception at the Salvation Army hostel, and mark it 'Private' as I can never be quite sure when you'll be at the library or when I'll be there myself, and this is an urgent matter. I'm sure your distinguished family, which will one day recover its fortunes, would know the importance of tact and discretion. It is a lovely, lovely birthday card and a lovely letter with it. Thank you. But, please, you MUST NOT push letters or cards through like that, even nice letters on genuine notepaper and in an envelope (I hope you did not splash out precious funds on stationery purposely) – which fortunately I found first among other mail on the mat. It is clear from this stationery that you were once used to 'the best'.

Your coming to the house would be very dangerous for me, plus the neighbours observing. I don't mean that in any way you are especially noticeable except, perhaps, for handsomeness – but people around us are ever watchful. Incidentally, do not telephone, either, please. There are many sophisticated devices here. Yes, I shall probably be visiting the library to continue my writing work off and on and it might well be possible to make contact.

Much love,
J

P.S. The weather does not seem really seasonal in my view – mild and cloudy. But perhaps this suits you and your colleagues.

49

Carthage
Tabbett Drive
Exall DL2 4NG

My dear Mother,

Having a little time on my hands, I thought I'd drop you a line so you have something to read in the 'dog days', as some, I believe, call this idle high-summer period. How worrying things must be for Mrs Cherie Blair in view of the attacks about their holidays. Meanwhile, her husband continues at the top despite Iraq and he is certainly always nicely turned out, his shirts pressed. But politics can swing about in a most baffling manner. Pre-marriage, she would have been Cherie Booth, which makes her sound like a little private room where you can get a shot of amontillado.

To date, as far as I can tell, it is still safe to address things to Mrs AV Ward, OBE. She has a degree of attraction, even without the gong, and despite burliness below. Dennis, the poor love, is really slaving away today, catching up again with letter writing on the word processor. This gives me a little time on my hands, but I have to be careful because the sound of the printer would drown his footsteps, especially on the beige fitted carpet. Should he materialize in his little way, I'll end and post this as it is (again!), because there will be little chance later owing to neighbourhood barbies and so on, and our weekend parties, which we maintain despite warm weather making for some breathlessness and discomfort, though a few actually find the extra sweatiness of a partner additionally entrancing. I feel it is this range of tastes – some entirely unexpected – that makes our Carthage get-togethers so worthwhile and constructive. Possibly, you will recall mention of a caftan bought deliberately by him for me as an offensive birthday present? I'm happy to say this was disposed of, finally. But, of course, he countered this and came up with another, just as foul, in time for my birthday. I have to say, he's got stickability, if nothing else, the twerp. Fortunately, I have been able to obtain a few gifts for his own birthday. I know I said I would not cheapen myself by retaliating, but how else can one respond if he does it twice, Mother? One of these is a leather-bound jotter for writing down your random thoughts etc, and titled a Commonplace Book printed in gold lettering, which attracted me since he is an Olympic standard commonplace.

What a strange pattern of events in those countries we used to call 'the Eastern Bloc'. Do you recall Mr Yeltsin who drank quite a lot, yet deserved better at the time? Now it's Putin, much thinner. We shall be having people in for one of our get-togethers this weekend, as a matter of fact. Salad is what I shall be serving, made with fine cos lettuces and other items, including tomatoes that really taste of something – so rare these days. I have to admit, though, it is probably not the food or drink that really draws people to these occasions! We try to keep everything comparatively mild in the summer because of the dangers of heart attacks, which brings us back to Mr Yeltsin. I felt concerned about his health from the start. He had such good intentions and yet the 'old guard' forces in that country were strong and disrespectful of what he tried to achieve. If we had heart attacks here at our home, it might not be too bad because one of our guests is herself a doctor, though there are matters of professional etiquette and all that, and guests who have seen her in one role at our evenings might not feel confident about her attentions in a professional way.

I've raised the matter of coming to you in the autumn and this was greeted with

50

Carthage

Dear Cindy,

It's very difficult to get hold of you by phone because of your busy medical duties, so I'm writing a line. Anyway, I do like putting nice things down on paper, sort of re-living them, and I feel you are one I can describe matters to in full. I don't know if you are familiar with that unpromising phrase 'a bit of rough', but there is a lot to be said for this kind of experience, in my view.

Dennis and I were really sorry you and Julian could not make our little 'get-together' the other weekend. It would really have made our day to have seen you again among our friends. This most recent party went reasonably well – general good fellowship, no violence or brutish noise, everyone ready to give and take as appropriate. Thongs are supposedly on the way out, but I don't know . . .

The future of democratic Iraq (as we must now call it!) still gives cause for anxiety, I fear, especially distrust and hatred between the various religious groups. There will be a continuing need for diplomatic effort.

I always refer to these days of July and August as 'the dog days', but at least the weather remains pleasant.

Some of our summer days here herald serious difficulties but one has to expect that from Dennis, I think, in a season of warmth and relaxation. It's his little way. I'll say this for him, although he is Gold Standard measly, he is not mean, and is ready to shell out when it comes to getting one of his paltry victories, which I suppose he did over the damn caftan, which I'm wearing now, due to birthday goodwill – such a powerful force. Fortunately, the public library reference room has become a real source of interesting contact. I have developed a heartening acquaintanceship there: fair-haired, worn in a ponytail, and lean. This is in addition to my other outside commitment, now beginning to flag, actually. Cindy, I don't know if you've ever had any sort of intimate experience in a library reference and reading room, but the excitement can be notable, as is the excitement now while I recall and write of it, I'm happy to say! Yes, one reason I like writing long letters is one gets to live things again . . .

Obviously, in the library, one has to take some care because people, bored with their heavy reading, may be gazing about, plus there are the attendants wandering around, fetching and carrying and keeping checks on books. However, this is one of the good, old-fashioned reading rooms, with very practical, long, heavy, leather-topped wooden tables, which cover so much, as you may recall, having studied a great deal to qualify. You can probably imagine or match some of the frights we've had. Cindy, even in summer some down-and-out visitors to the library do need additional comforting in their threadbare,

Oxfam, pinstripe trousers. The particular excitement springs, and owes much I believe, to the prevailing bookishness and mahogany dignity of the library reading room, from which these moments might reasonably be deemed an escape, I would say – an escape without actually leaving the building!

Apart from the library, the summer has been notable for various social calls, to and from neighbours and friends in a spirit of great camaraderie (do you know this pretty word?). Obviously, one's mind is also on parts of the world where the peacefulness and joy of the day are unavailable, such as Iraq, scene of continual bloody strife. And then there's the Middle East from time to time – *always* the Middle East from time to time. Nonetheless, it is possible to derive abiding joy and strength from a glorious summer despite Dennis.

Mrs AV Ward, OBE, and her uninspiring husband, Eric, were among those who called on us, and I was very glad, for we do owe them much hospitality, quite apart from a personal debt I have to her. Dennis brought out some quite fine Pouilly-Fumé, which is what I mean about eschewing meanness, a lovely side to him, and only in part due to an interest in Mrs Ward, and a pathetic determination to impress. Her hubby, ugly and getting on for debilitated, seems one for 'turning the blind eye', and is, I believe, rather fearful of her, even before the OBE in her own right. This visit was not, of course, to one of our weekend events but a private supper for the four of us.

Do let me know how your own and Julian's summer is going – your own, perhaps, with increased activity at A and E, what with sunburn, drink-driving through heat thirst, nervous breakdowns from terrorism fears, barbecue glassings and general greed with fruit. Old films in these wasteland days are a treat, but why did Harry Lime invite Joseph Cotton over from the US to Vienna if Harry knew he was going to pretend to be dead and buried? We can't ask Graham Greene any longer. Harry would surely know his friend was likely to start digging, as it were, which would not be what Harry wanted at all. Is *The Third Man* really one of the best films ever made? I doubt

Dennis would think so, it not being an Alain Delon masterpiece!

The present tally of invitations to late summer parties is three, but still counting, thanks to Dennis's general, gratifying acceptability in the neighbourhood and beyond. His shallowness allows the charm to be very near the surface in his little way. He wants Mrs AV Ward invited to one of our weekend things, for obvious reasons, but I'm against, absolutely. For a start we've never brought neighbours in to that sort of thing. You cannot be sure what their long-term reactions might be, and I have to meet them in shops and so on in quite different guises. Or they could start going on about lowering the quality of the neighbourhood etc and ring Environmental Health anonymously. For some of them, talking about the quality of the neighbourhood is their long suit. Again, I'm not having that Eric here in those circumstances, going sheepish and with his dismaying cough. Also, I believe an OBE might cast a pall. People would grow self-conscious, even our liberated 'regulars' although, obviously she would not be wearing it. In fact, I can tell you now, Cindy, that having a practising doctor at our weekends gave me an anxiety or two originally, but I need not have fretted because you adapted so fluently. I think adaptability is your long suit. I know Dennis would wish me to pass on his warmest to you and Julian for the rest of the summer, and I do for myself, of course. Please do not hesitate to let us know if you want topiary in any form, perhaps some notable medical scientist like Madam Curie.

Looking forward to our next meeting,

Jill

51

Carthage
Tabbett Drive
Exall DL2 4NG
Wednesday

My dear Mother,

Well, here we are, nearly three-quarters of the way through the fifth year of this new millennium! Perhaps, though, it's not so new any longer. Who knows how many more years we'll be granted, things having turned out the way they have, with the street violence, climate change and the very unstable situation in all kinds of trouble spots such as the Middle East – always the Middle East.

We both hope you are having a wonderful summer, and we are sure you are, knowing your capacity for enjoying yourselves. Here, everything has been extremely pleasant and merry, with Dennis at his very wonderful best in a fancy dress party at the club. We went as the Babes in the Wood, Dennis wanting nothing to do with any characters from TV, regarding them all as a 'cheap cliché'. Dennis is one with admirably strong and clear views.

We had leaves stuck to our fetching twill costumes, signifying being lost in the woods and sleeping there under a covering of leaves. Many recognized at once the roles we had taken, and we were awarded a notable prize. An atmosphere of cheerfulness and grand optimism re. the future pervaded the whole evening, and this heartened everyone. I kept my eyes open, obviously. This club, The Alexandria, is very select and panelled but has all sorts of little rooms in it, and there were times when I lost track of Dennis and Veronica – as she is these days – and I think her husband was looking, too. He came as a miner, with smudges, a lamp and helmet, poor thing, though the lamp was not in working order to help him find her, of course, and Veronica herself looked really lovely as what I believe was known as an Air Raid Precautions warden during the war, also with a helmet and in navy dungarees, plus gas mask satchel. Epaulets displayed the letters in gold, ARP, and imparted flair. Dungarees are not cut too tight, and so good for someone heavyish below. She is really clever and honest about acknowledging her bad aspects, and dunga-rees would come off easily enough, I expect, or there would not have been so much famous 'carrying on' in air-raid shelters in the war.

As the sole OBE in The Alexandria during the party, Mrs AV Ward was allowed to introduce the few speeches, and performed this with fine, prolonged dignity and wit. Presence is one of her finest aspects. Also, her duties involved leading the singing of various oldie numbers, which she performed with true panache.

Mentions of my proposed visit to you are not greeted by him with favour. He wishes to know all proposed details, and to be given a full statement of the reasons for the visit. He says he reserves the right, if I go, to telephone your house at random times, particularly during the night, and possibly repeatedly, to ensure that I am safely in. Randomness is one of his long suits. This, in its lousy way, is gratifying, even a kind of caring, but could also be trying.

Arrangements with a different bank from our usual one are underway to acquire the facility of a locked box in their deposit room, in which I wish to place a statement with particular reference to threats etc. When I have completed arrangements with the bank I'll send you an authorization to open in certain eventualities and, of course, a key.

We are much enjoying the still, long days, though a shortening is certainly perceptible. Together, we sit at home in the upstairs bay window and jointly savour the beautiful evenings. It is a gratifying experience and we are jointly moved.

Also, you may have seen they've been reviving that serial on television called *Clarissa*, that I mentioned a while ago. It is a girl's story which was originally told completely in letters, an interesting method, which used to be the style of many novels, concerning the danger she was in – i.e. rape. Of course, there was no pill or phone then or 999, and girls definitely had to worry more. I've always believed, as you know, that letters can say so much. My own view is, Clarissa should not have spent so much time writing, but used the time to plan how to snuff him out and escape the stock female rôle of victim.

Dennis, I know, would wish to join with me in wishing you once more all the very best and in thanking you for all your kindnesses, especially the remarkably coherent references to the Alain Delon films for him, you not being experts.

Your loving daughter,
Jill

52

Carthage

Dearest Greg,

Darling, honestly, that can happen to any man once in a while and, as I said, you must not be distressed. You say it is anxiety, which I regard as so typically modest of you, for I believe there is little that could really frighten you, and certainly not a supposedly anonymous letter from him, or the possible presence of some snoop, or of him snooping himself – he would really enjoy that, he's a born spy. You've doubtless heard of borrowed time. What he's on, in my opinion.

Please, please, don't ever talk again about the possibility of our discontinuing. My distress at such a prospect becomes a turmoil, as you witnessed, and I am sorry for talking and behaving as I did. I honestly wish to thank you for bringing me under control again. Never would I do you any real injury, though. Let me assure you again – and again and again – that my violence in no way resulted from contemptuous rage at your failure. It was wholly a display of pain at the notion of losing you. You are the essence of my life and I would be finished if we were ever to become permanently separated.

He took the opportunity, when we were with friends lately and he had had a few gins, to talk maudlinly to them of the 'glorious' years together which were in prospect for him and me, not just immediately but 'deep into the twenty-first century'. He has this undoubted gift of the gab and, as he spoke, sensible people suddenly struck up with 'For They Are Jolly Good Fellows', meaning him and me, but as he maundered I heard a knell.

Our fine friend will soon re-emerge alert and bonny from his laundered lair, don't worry, like Sredni Vashtar, that ferocious, sleek, god-like polecat in the Saki story you read me so tellingly once. Literature's got such a stack of juicy symbols, hasn't it? That's the limits of him, hired snoops, insolent caftans and notes in capitals. He can't last.

I'll be there on Sunday again.

Your loving,
Jill

53

My dear Peregrine,

I am addressing this to you at the hostel marked 'Private', and I hope you are still spending some time there and get it. I intend to deliver it by hand. You will forgive me for not putting an address on the notepaper, owing to the danger of the letter 'going astray' and I do not want DIFFICULTIES from returned mail marked 'Gone Away' and so on.

Please do not feel hurt re. the following, but you must *not* telephone here again, lovely as it was to hear your dear voice – and obviously almost entirely unjuiced, which shows grand restraint and consideration, Perry. Well done! You must not waste your funds with such calls, which I have perforce to ring off from instantly, and it is extremely dangerous for me, owing to all sorts of devices here. As it is, I am not sure what he will make of it, though I rang off so instantly, you having spoken my name and possibly your own. I'm sorry about that, but I am very exposed, believe me. Also, although it was very pleasant to see you close by in Tabbett Drive, I feel it is unwise for you to wait about there, as you did on both Saturday and Sunday. I have mentioned this to you before. Neighbours here have considerable idleness and the time to be very observant. Also, they are sharp at putting two and two together. One of my neighbours, a full OBE, is extremely sensitive about suggestiveness and marital impropriety from others. The ponytail (which, as you well know, I adore) and your delightful, fun waistcoat would probably make you stand out in this hopelessly staid area. At weekends, I perforce spend a great deal of time jointly with my hubbie, thus there is *no* possibility that I would be able to join you, owing to joint outings taken by my hubbie and myself, or people visiting us socially, when it would be impossible for me to ask you in from Tabbett Drive as an acquaintance fortuitously spotted there, owing to all the explaining required and their pronounced 'cliqueyness' believe me.

I think, in fact Perry, darling, that matters have to be faced, and we must call an end. This you will say is a sudden decision, after such lovely recent times, and in a way you are right. But there are sudden pressures. It is clearly impossible to go to the dear, dear old library in the present conditions, with that odious woman threatening to bring in police, and possibly a newspaper reporter, out of basic malice. This could become rather difficult, especially were your distinguished family name to be blazoned across some tabloid rag for alleged improper actions. In fact, dear Perry, I have a very full life to lead, thus am not really in a position to undertake any long-term, new directions with you. I feel sure that very soon you and your colleagues will wish to be on the move anyway, and, of course, at any time you may hear from your distinguished family that the potential inheritance is now in place, furnishing extensive, cattle-rich acres, meres and the manor house. At that point, I have no doubt you will wish to return to the Avers-Lancing and, doubtless, in time, select a fortunate girl of your own sort to wed and furnish lineage after your brave, mind-extending look at the rougher sides of life in the mode of that famous writer, Orwell, you mentioned once, showing me a book of his in the library about the 'down and out' life. Books are so useful.

It makes me sad to write this, but I must perforce face it. Your future wife will have much that I will miss. Thus, this is a final goodbye, Perry, dear, which I do hope you will definitely accept, and I do hope also that you take care of yourself and are able to fend off the bad weather when it comes. So far, fortunately, the beautiful summer continues, but we are well over the longest day and on our way to autumn. Perhaps the winter will be mild. I do hope so. I would like to believe that you will think of me sometimes, wherever you are, and that you will continue to reduce your cider intake, at which you were becoming wonderfully successful, despite the foolishly mocking attitude of Heavy Royston and Bert, whom, in my view, you would be better off without, and who anyone could see have negligible family backgrounds, if that. Their attitude to books in the reading room was flippant to say the least.

Owing to the chance that this letter might 'go astray', I did not think it wise to include money, but I have paid a certain sum in cash at the Rich Pickings café in Dale Street and been assured that this will cover at least ten standard lunches or dinners (midday or evening). Please do not feel too proud to go there, nor I hope will you regard this gesture as a cold, severance pay-off. I told the proprietor that you would identify yourself as being entitled and he assured me *in person* that there would be absolutely no difficulty about allocating a table. Please spread these meals out over a period, thus getting regular nourishment. I have heard independently their goulash is exceptionally good value with meat aplenty, and I only wish we could jointly eat out there, but this, alas, can never be, not in this life, anyway!

Yours with fondest memories,

J

54

PEREGRINE-BLOODY-AVERS-BLOODY-LANCING-ESQ. IS IT?
I'VE GOT YOU VERY NOTED MY OLD LAYABOUT.

55

Dear Tim,

Your letter just received, and thank you for being so under-standing and, indeed, patient in the matter of the caftans, on which I fear I may have 'spread myself' rather. It is kind of you to note that there is a real point at issue here, not simply some petty rattiness or panic on my part. Tim, another seemingly small event occurred shortly after I had sealed my last letter which you might also consider – as I do, I fear – to have implications that are worrying and, yes, enraging.

A grand summer has spread pleasant feelings in our home and those of our neighbours. In good sunshine, local differ-ences can be forgotten. Many visitors called on us for alfresco meals, and we in turn on them. I will say this for Jill and her brazenness, Tim, she took the caftan business extremely calmly, reacting without obvious frenzy at the appearance of the replacement on her birthday morn, and exclaiming delightedly about its style and colours, then unforcedly donning it on several occasions since. As I expected, no mention has been made of the swap of the first one, and, naturally, in my turn, I will react with extreme civility to the gifts she has no doubt devilishly picked out for my birthday.

111

But Tim, what happened a few days ago was that Jill went out in the early evening, prior to a small, extremely pleasant, even distinguished, party we attended later. Professional surveillance now being at least suspended and perhaps concluded, I thought it might be a challenge to follow her myself, seeking to remain unobserved. I decided to regard this quite light-heartedly, as a kind of summer game, like a paperchase, for instance. I think, if I may say so, I managed it extremely well, and she does not know I watched her. Imagine my surprise, Tim, when the destination for Jill turned out to be not some gratification rendezvous by car, but the Salvation Army hostel in Wellington Gardens. This she entered briefly, apparently leaving something at the reception desk, which I could only only assume to be a donation to their funds. About this she had said nothing to me, and I at first felt it to be a lovely gesture, one which made me wonder whether I had been wrongly thinking ill of her and unfairly building to anger. There are some wonderful sides to her personality, obviously, and it seemed heartening, sitting there, watching her from the car, to be reminded of her strengths and generosity. Little did I realize, however, what I was to discover.

Tim, when she left I thought it best to check my impression of the situation and entered the reception office on the pretext of asking for directions. The envelope she had brought was resting on top of papers in a tray, and I could see it was addressed in her handwriting to Peregrine Avers-Lancing Esqre. – that Esqre. thing she read in some ancient etiquette book. When I said something facetious about the elaborateness of this name and suggested it must be someone important, such as the director of the hostel, the receptionist had a short, harsh guffaw, Tim, and said this Peregrine Avers-Lancing was one of their 'in and out guests' as he termed it, well known around the Central Gardens and public library, and not for carrying 'For God So Loved The World' sandwich boards or reading devotional works, either. I had already heard something about suspected unkempt behaviour by Jill in the public library reading room, and the receptionist's reply caused me great hurt and anger, naturally. I remain mystified and perturbed.

Several times during the 'barbie season' I saw the woman neighbour whom I have already mentioned to you, but her husband stayed very, very close, I thought, hands-on spouse-manship, perhaps having sniffed something, the way they do. Maybe I should say, the way *we* do. He's dozey, but not that dozey, so the conversation had to be restricted to this neighbour's OBE and her good works, which are very genuine, heart-warming and extensive. However, I shall keep the arrangement on the back burner.

May the pleasant summer continue, Tim, and may you enjoy it to the full,

Your brother,
Dennis.

56

Carthage
Tabbett Drive
Exall DL2 4NG
23 August 2005

Dear Anna,

Obviously I have not received your reply to my last letter yet, but – on the kind of topic I was discussing there – I would like to offer a small postscript about something that happened after I had sealed my previous letter. I don't think you will feel I'm making 'mountains out of molehills' either in this matter of the caftans. All of it illustrates only too well, I fear, the state of affairs with which I have to contend, and which may well force me to a major decision soon, though I hope one not taken in the temporary irrationality of fury.

A grand summer has spread pleasant feelings in our home and those of our neighbours. In good sunshine, local differences can be forgotten. Many visitors called on us for alfresco meals . . .

. . . I remain mystified and perturbed.

I will say no more now, having already in these letters spent too long boring you with my 'troubles'.

Fondly,
Dennis

57

Carthage
Tabbet Drive
Exhall DL2 4NG
23 August 2005

Dear Marie,

I have not received your reply to my last letter yet, but – on the kind of topic I was discussing there – I would like to offer a small postscript about something that happened after I had sealed my previous letter. I believe it to be extremely relevant to the anxieties you expressed about the depth of my commitment here. I don't think you will feel I'm making 'mountains out of molehills' either in this matter of the caftans. All of it illustrates only too well, I fear, the state of affairs with which I have to contend, and which may well force me to a major decision soon, though I hope one not taken in the temporary irrationality of fury.

A grand summer has spread pleasant feelings in our home and those of our neighbours. In good sunshine, local differences can be forgotten. Many visitors called on us for alfresco meals . . .

. . . I remain mystified and perturbed.

I will say no more now, having already in these two letters spent too long boring you with my 'troubles'.

All my love, dear Marie,

Dennis

58

Memo:
Date: **25 August 2005**
From: **Susan Wright (counsellor)**
To: **Catherine Wilberforce (supervisor)**

With reference to your memo asking whether there have been further developments in the case of client AVW, I have to report that she has not reappeared for counselling since my original memo on 27 June and that I therefore have no further information.

SW

25 August 2005

59

Dear Tim,

It could be that you are right and I persist almost obsessively with more and more research into Jill's behaviour, instead of committing myself to action. Yes, I agree with you, the detective's reports could not be more conclusive or enraging, and then the revelations at the Salvation Army hostel. I was nervous at the time about committing photocopies of the detective's reports to the post for you, but am now very glad I took the risk and can profit from your views.

I suppose what stalls me is the recollection of that other fearful business, and the guilt and anxiety which came, I think, to both of us after that – certainly to me. It's a long time ago and perhaps we can be confident it will never bring us trouble now. But this is partly the point concerning Jill. I can't believe one could have the kind of luck that allows one to get away with such a previous incident; and then would again be able to escape the consequences of something so very similar. I'm talking about the law of averages.

Yet, you will reasonably ask in reply, what is the point of amassing this kind of unambiguous material about her behaviour if I do not at some stage act? But those words 'at some stage' are crucial, Tim. I do assure you that there will come a point when ... Well, the point will come, doubt not.

Please don't take this amiss, but I would still prefer to handle the situation personally. It is kind and typical of you to offer to come down and help – selflessly to accept, as ever, the responsibilities of older brother – and I do understand your anger after reading the reports and hearing subsequent information. Yes, they do taint not just me but our dear family, in the widest sense. I, too, feel such anger, clearly, Tim. This anger will endure and will in due course find proper expression, believe me.

Yours,
Dennis

60

Carthage
Tabbett Drive
Exall DL2 4NG
28 August 2005

My dear Mother,

Just the briefest of notes to say that I am quite well and that things seem to be going not too badly. Hearing children in the street talk about going back after the holidays, I began to wonder for a while about the education prospects in this country. Class size is a much debated topic, yet to these children school is just school, I should think, and a pain. Private education does not seem so much a matter of controversy as it once was. I sometimes wonder whether all that bullying in *Tom Brown's Schooldays* is really a thing of the past, as maintained by supporters of public schools.

Thinking of schools, I believe I mentioned that a friend who was in the same class as me has begun attending our weekend get-togethers with her hubbie? She seems to enjoy herself considerably, and has made a mark on some of our other guests. But her husband is prim and ill-made, with deadbeat bits of what he thinks are wit. Dennis is inclined to ask how I have this friend or that friend, as if my life only started when I met him. It is as though he thinks he created me and owns me, like one of his dear monstrosities made of leaves. Arrogance is his long suit. I give him wholly friendly and full answers because I know my time will eventually come. One day this prince will learn there's more to life than privet. As a matter of fact, he is admirably and bustlingly busy now on the hedge and his little stepladder is really taking a hammering, but in such a good cause.

I'm glad to say I feel considerably relaxed because of his recent harmony, yet always remaining alert, fear not. Stress has subsided, knowing he is occupied and in his drab little way content. I will close, wishing to tune in to a late night discussion on, as a matter of fact, education reforms. May I wish you, as ever, on behalf of Dennis and myself all the very best.

Your loving daughter,
Jill

61

Carthage
Tabbit Drive
Exall DL2 4NG
29 August 2005

Dear Mr Lavery,

Thank you for your recent letters and for the kind offer in your second letter of reduced rates for whom you so flatteringly call 'an esteemed and established client'. But I'm afraid I must abide by my original decision and terminate our arrangement, without the least reflection intended on the operations of your agency or, specifically, of Mr JJP Nelmes. All the essential work has, indeed, been carried out – and admirably carried out – by Mr Nelmes, and anything remaining to be done is merely confirmatory: i.e. the Volvo and private house assignations and certain other sorties which have developed lately. The follow-up to all these I sincerely believe I can adequately handle myself, and I have already conducted one or two operations quite successfully, I venture to think, and without being detected.

I really am grateful for your kind and understanding words, and please rest assured that should I need further assistance I shall call on your admirable firm again.

Yours sincerely,
DJ Seagrave

62

Fairholm
Tabbett Drive
Exall DL2 5NG
29 August 2005

RD Simms
UN Emergency Force
PO Box 71
Central Africa

Dear Rowena,

Thanks so much for your news-filled letters and for the congrats on the medal. I really was not at all sure about accepting it. I mean, when I think of people doing the kind of work you are handling out there, and without much recognition, it seemed almost absurd to take the OBE. However, I did and there was quite a party here – but more of that shortly. Yes, indeed. Some of the conditions you describe sound appalling and you write of them with a terrible graphicness that matches anything we see on TV.

I do wish you were nearer, so I might consult you, seek your advice. Confession: things have moved on between myself and the hub of the neighbour who receives her letters here. He will be D in any mentions I make. I'm afraid I did/do find him irresistible, so decisive and yet with a creative turn, also, and eventually (or sooner than that, actually) the inevitable occurred and continues wonderfully to occur. Things began to get warm on the night of the OBE fest, as a matter of fact. Pressure on all bloody sides, of course. First, I have to worry about Eric, who is particularly sharp on spotting this sort of thing (he saw something was 'on' between David and Penny, you'll recall, when nobody else had noticed, and when I wouldn't have believed it if I had). Second, my lady neighbour, J, is a brain, despite some of her silly ways and talk, and I have to fret about what she might suspect. Thank goodness Donna is away at school still, because she's pretty perceptive, too.

Third, and what brings the major worries, are these damn letters I receive for D's wife. I've stayed quiet about them to D so far. But they obviously put me in a spot. It seems wrong now, in the changed circumstances, to keep that kind of secret from him. Really two-faced. All right, I'm two-faced already, I know, by having the relationship, but to mention nothing about this correspondence would seem to make things very much worse. What I really worry about is the possibility that he should find out by some other means that I help his wife in this way. How would he think of me then, Rowena? Deceit upon deceit. There is an undisclosed side to him, exciting but also very dark, I think, and I would certainly not like to cross him.

And so, I am greatly inclined to tell him of the postal arrangement. I would, of course, never allow him to open the letters, or even see and touch them. But I would like to get the basic burden of secrecy and deception off my shoulders. Do you think it would be wise to reveal that much to him?

I've said little about the positive side. I have found nothing about D on better acquaintance (much better!) that contradicts my initial favourable feelings, except for this sense of shadow somewhere in his being. If one can forget that – and I can for most of the time – he is a gem, and he's mine, Rowena. Or he's mine when we are together. He's due to go to London again shortly in connection with some continuing film research, or that's the tale, anyway, and I feel quite down at the thought of separation, even for a short while. Perhaps what I've called the undisclosed side of him is something brutal in his past somewhere. That's just an impression. It could be nothing. Anyway, it does bring an aura, and any kind of aura makes a change after Eric.

All my love,
Veronica (for now)

63

Gregory R Patterson,
14A Hill Park,
Exall DB7 4SB
29 August 2005

Dear Steve,

Have been trying to get you by phone but you never seem to be in. Could you give me a call at home or in work? I might need a job reference, if you could manage it, please. I'm looking fairly urgently for a decent post abroad. Coopers & Lybrand have been advertising for corporate finance management consultants in Africa. Things are turning rather hairy here in the situation we've discussed previously. Don't get me wrong, I'm still deeply committed, but there are some new and nasty complications – e.g. he knows, and things could get messy. A couple of times after a few drinks I've found myself discussing quite monstrous solutions to the problems here.

Hope all's well with the business school.

Yours,
Greg

64

My dear Mother,

Isn't it terrible about New Orleans? How close we all live to chaos every day. I have just this moment returned from Mrs AV Ward, OBE's, where I was able to read, re-read and re-re-read your letter prior to disposal. This facility is heartening at such unpredictable times. As you say, we are nearing autumn now, and I have certainly mentioned to my friend Cindy not to blab about her weekend times here, as we don't want all sorts wishing to come, especially in the approaching dark nights when too many unlit parked cars in Tabbett Drive for very long stretches can be a desperate nuisance and very obvious. Dennis is a great believer in consideration for the neighbours, no matter how slobby some of them are. Music is always kept low in volume, etc., and we are very discreet with any special refuse that has to be put out. Cindy, a full medical doctor despite everything, is accustomed to confidentiality.

He is going away briefly again to research some matters to do with his Delon concordance, alleged. There's remarkable energy about him, I'll admit that. Loneliness in dear Denn's absence does not greatly bug me, as I am able to use the time for thinking about topics that might get neglected in the usual hurly-burly of life. Almost meditation! For instance, on the economic front the signs remain confusing, don't they, while Africa and various terrible famines still cause concern. I thought of going into the park to write this as he

Later

And perhaps I should have. Certain pressures. But it really is all right. Don't grow anxious, please. How time flies, though, doesn't it? Please don't think I'm sweeping the matter of the visit under the carpet.

Love to both,
Jill.

65

Perdita Close
1 September 2005

My dear Jill,

Your father and I feel so desperately helpless. Your letters make us terribly anxious, yet there seems nothing we can do. Are you sure we should not visit you right away? I do not mean, necessarily, that we should stay at your home. We could go to an hotel and call on you as and when convenient. We have come to hate to think of you isolated there. We hardly recognize the man you describe as Dennis, yet we have to believe what you write. We hate to think of you in constant fear – afraid even to write your lovely letters at home and often forced instead to the public library at the risk of brutish fingers.

If it would be unwise to come to visit you, why should you not come here for a while? You keep saying it is inconvenient, but surely he could not object to a visit to your own parents? Father even suggests that you do not discuss it with him, but simply come, and tell him by phone when you arrive. I don't think I'd go along with that, but you will see the kind of extreme uneasiness which grips your father and, indeed, myself.

I do so dislike this arrangement of writing to you via Mrs AV Ward. Of course, I am extremely grateful that she should provide this facility. Yet I am bound to worry about the confidentiality of the arrangement, particularly as you suggest an 'understanding' might develop at any time between her and Dennis.

But we will, of course, continue to behave in whichever way seems to you safest and most apt. Do, though, keep us informed. We love your letters and the occasional calls from public phone booths. Above all, dear, take care.

Your loving mother

66

Carthage
4 September 2005

Dear Tim,

I'm just back from London and in many respects feel really restored. When in this mood, I wonder sometimes whether my troubles have finally ended – even wonder sometimes whether they were imaginary, though, of course, there is a ton of evidence to suggest not.

No, I have received no reply from Anna yet. It's possible, even likely, that I never shall. Perhaps the address I have is out of date. Perhaps she does not wish to be bothered with the distant troubles of someone who passed out of her life years ago, and in sad circumstances. She has made something new for herself, and I'm sure is totally happy. It might activate old feelings, old pains, to put herself in touch with me again, or with either of us. Perhaps it is best if we regard that fierce, rough-house chapter in our lives as over. And perhaps she has decided this, too.

I'm not at all sure what went on here in my absence because I have dispensed with surveillance. You know how it is, I expect, when someone has been in your home again, the fact unacknowledged? It is a sickening notion that an outsider should have been sitting secretly in this favourite chair or furtively handling books lovingly collected and cared for – as if vandals had intruded. I'm not one to go snooping for traces, I hope. It's simply a question of the build up of affront and revulsion. I assure you I shall do nothing precipitate. That's not my way now, I assure you. But you know this.

Your brother,
Dennis

67

If the Seagraves were to sell up and go – and still no real evidence of that, in fact, no evidence at all – it would probably be because of boredom. I've always feared that for them Tabbett Drive is a backwater – quiet and pleasant, sure, but not what two childless folk like Jill and Dennis are after, perhaps. Between them they confer so much on the Drive. But what do they get from it?

In part I think the fault is their own. Although they do participate in some of the local life – coffee mornings, fêtes, parties – they give the impression of being fairly apart from things. They will turn up to these occasions from time to time, but there is no real enthusiasm. Perhaps they are wrapped up in each other, even now after being married for so long.

*Well, if that's so, good luck to them, says I. Such content-
ment is rare enough, Lord knows.*

*Just the same, I feel a sort of debt. Somehow they bring
an aura to the Drive and, in return, I would like to
discourage them from going. Perhaps with the help of a
few neighbours who agree we might be able to do something. On the other hand, the whole tale about a move is
possibly only that, a tale. I sometimes feel it has become
a little* over *polite not to ask them if it is true. But might
it be regarded as prying? I would hate to get known as
Neighbourhood Watch.*

68

Fairholm
8 September 2005

RD Simms
UN Emergency Force
PO Box 71
Central Africa

My dear Rowena,

Thanks again – and again – for your brilliant phone calls.
Oh, it is wonderful to hear your voice across all those miles.
You are entirely unboastful, yet I still get the impression of
magnificent intrepidity. Even Eric grows excited when your
calls come, so, on top of your work for humanity out there,
you are achieving a take-up-your-bed-and-walk miracle here.
Although they were, of course, spoken with marvellous
discretion and in general terms, I did get the gist of your

warnings about my own activities, and I am grateful for them, absolutely.

As a matter of fact, they chime with some of my own thoughts. Things certainly continue as before, but I have been made uneasy now and then. I don't really know why, but I get the impression of some sort of mounting crisis at my neighbour's house – I mean something really out of control, and obviously a situation I must on no account get drawn into. I think such was the kind of possibility you were hinting at skillfully in your second call, and you sharpened into real awareness what, up until then, had been only my vague apprehension. I have Donna as well as Eric to consider.

In social groups, the neighbours seem totally happy together, even over-considerate and charming, yet I do feel I pick up a ferocious reciprocal . . . what? Suspicion of each other? Hate of each other? Is that OTT? Perhaps they blame each other for the lack of children. Perhaps . . . but perhaps almost anything. In his references to her when alone with me, D is usually cool but not vindictive. I still haven't had the nerve to ask him about the occasional weekend things at their house. Best to be very careful with him. He erects this barrier between us, and very much behind it are concealed some things from his past, and some from now.

What especially worries me, Ro, is the impression I get – I seem to be full of impressions, no certainties – that he knows about the letter-drop arrangement. All my agonizings over whether I would be able to keep quiet about it might be crazy. The other day, for instance, he said something like, 'Of course my wife's often popping in here, isn't she, for one thing or the other? You do help her a lot.' Well, I said something about cups of sugar, but he just stared. He's frighteningly good at staring, and sometimes I must admit I can see why she might be scared of him: rather small, hard eyes, yet not unattractive, obviously, or why would I be drawn to him? But how *could* he know about the letters, Rowena? All I can think is, he might somehow have managed a look at one of her letters describing the arrangement. But D certainly does not seem to me the sort who would read another person's letter, snoop on someone. I could not stand a man like that.

And then something really horrible came to me, horrible and so hurtful, Ro. Tell me how it strikes you. This is a youngish, very attractive man. I am a middle-ageish, fattish OBE. Is he only interested in me because he's curious about the letters that come here for her? Will he ask to see them one day? He hasn't yet, and has never even spoken of them in plain terms. But I do wonder, wonder and weep, Rowena. He is clever and he probably knows how to be patient. It would, obviously, mean he was simply using me, but also show that his real concern is still with *her*, and for the sake of that, he will go to bed with *me*. If he ever does ask to see those letters, I think I shall just disintegrate.

I don't feel like writing any more now. Look after yourself.

Love,
Alice

69

Gregory R Patterson
14A Hill Park
Exall DB7 4SB
8 September 2005

HL Sanderson
Head of Games and Leisure Activity
Weald Collegiate.

Dear Harry,

I'm writing to ask whether you could let me have a reference for use with a job application. I'm in for a couple of financial consultancy posts in Africa, and am required to provide not just a testimonial as to my professional abilities but something about my general character and social being. Maybe this side of things is important if one is in a comparatively small community of exiles. You'll remember that (thanks, of course, to your admirable coaching!) I became a capable rugby flanker and, in fact, captained the 1st XV in my second and third years. I imagine these are the kind of team and leadership qualities that would be relevant. I also did a lot of tennis, range shooting and chess and was vice-captain of the water polo side in my last year. In addition, any general remarks about my affability, honesty, reliability, charm, wit and, naturally, sobriety would be useful. They'll want to be sure I'm not in danger of 'going to the bad' out there.

I've been very happy here, but feel one ought to apply

one's trained skills to aiding a Third World emergent nation, at least for a few years. Hope all's well with you.

Yours,

Gregory R Patterson

70

Carthage

My dearest Mother,

Well, autumn definitely approaches and no more happy celebrations until Yule. I've been wondering whether to take that caftan (mark 2) out secretly one night and hang it on the clothes line of someone I detest, so neighbours assume it's hers and get a true giggle.

I don't think you should worry too much about Mrs AV Ward OBE (Order of the Bum Enormous). They've almost definitely got something going, those two – can't you always just *smell* something like that when two people are in company, trying to act so cool? But I don't believe she could tell him about the letters or she would be in a dicey spot, wouldn't she? I mean, even if she said she started it before *they* started it (!), it would still be a plot against him. And, if she knows him at all – which she ought to by now, thanks to their nooky twice a week – she would realize this might turn him damn malevolent.

Still these arguments about Europe and our involvement. Yes, poor Sir Edward Heath, so disappointed in his later days, having been the architect of much of this country's positive attitude to Europe. I'm not surprised his voice used to get throaty when chivvied about it on *Newsnight*. I notice voices. I should think he spoke all kinds of foreign tongues, being so European, but it must make it difficult with a throaty voice like that, except for German, maybe, which always sounds throaty whoever is speaking it. That *achtung* you hear in Nazi dramas on TV is like someone getting ready to spit.

Dennis, I know, would certainly like to be remembered to you and Father and we look forward to seeing you both when it is timely.

Your loving daughter,
Jill

71

Dear Greg,

Tried your office phone, but got only that snotty, snooty, brick-walling cow in reception. You're not doing something fleshly there, are you? She sounds damn jealous and possessive. What does she look like? And today only your answerphone at home and voicemail on the mobile. Just the same, I wanted to send a line to say how wonderful it was last night (again!). I think you're wonderfully brave not to worry about what D must know and what his knowledge might do to his gross, scheming mind. It is a situation in which we must both accept the dark hazards. *Malheureusement*, I grow tremulous now and then, and it's always a tonic to see how constant and unshaken you remain. I was going to deposit, with a substantial neighbour, a written statement of how things are/were here, in case of accidents and for opening only in an eventuality, of course. But I'm not so sure of this now, owing to the certainty of something between them, and not just hedges! Possibly any such note would get opened jointly and ruthlessly for their own damn pry purposes *before* the eventuality. I could hire a personal locked box at the bank instead, though, *malheureusement*, he knows people there and they might sing to him. It is definitely necessary, though, to consider applying eventualities ourselves *very*, *very* soon. I've just come across this French word *malheureusement*, which seems much more expressive than 'unfortunately'. We have to think European, don't we?

Soon, my love,
J

72

27 Perdita Close
Amberchase
Lancs
12 September 2005

Dear Mrs AV Ward,

As you can see, I have delayed for a very long time in replying to your letter. Frankly, I was not certain how to deal with it. If you remember, I had asked you if you, as a neighbour to my daughter, knew whether her fears of her husband were real or imagined. You did not appear to answer this point and I decided that perhaps you had deliberately avoided the matter, for fear of becoming involved in what should be a strictly private, family concern. I could understand that.

Yet I find I cannot let things lie in this way. My husband and I are so confused, so distressed. We have to take Jill's letters as being true. We particularly have to accept as binding her warnings not to visit, because this might make things worse for her. But if she is only imagining these perils, we are obviously doing her husband a terrible injustice, and we are neglecting our daughter, for she must be in need of medical or psychiatric care. Possibly, we are the only ones who realize this. She might be keeping up a different front with her husband. My reluctance to write again has also been affected by the fact that some of what conceivably are only her imaginings affect you, Mrs Ward. I will not elaborate upon them now, but you can understand, perhaps, that they place me in a worrying position.

However, you are the only person I can approach for help and so I am writing again. I remain extremely grateful for your kindness in providing the letter service, and, indeed, the general support to Jill. Might I, though, earnestly ask you to give me your opinion on whether or not my daughter is mentally sick or is in real peril? Her marriage seems to continue well enough despite her seeming fears, so we are sadly baffled over how to think and act.

Yours sincerely,
Gwen Day (Mrs)

73

Gregory R Patterson
14A Hill Park
Exall DB7 4SB
12 September 2005

Dear Steve,

A note to say that I'm through what they call the 'paper sieve' for the Africa job and have been for a first interview, from which they form their short list. I'm sure the success so far is all due to your ecstatic reference, for which many thanks. I do wish things could move quicker, though. Matters here really do grow tense. Not all of them, I understand, but those that do scare me rigid – or unrigid in one or two (well, three) instances. I've considered just getting out anyway, new job or not. It's that bad. Will keep you in the picture.

Yrs,
Greg

74

Gregory R Patterson
14A Hill Park
Exall DB7 4SB
12 September 2005

HL Sanderson
Head of Games and Leisure Activity
Weald Collegiate

Dear Harry,

A note to say that I'm through what they call the 'paper sieve' for the Africa job and have been for a first interview, from which they form their short list. I'm sure the success so far is all due to your ecstatic reference, for which many thanks. In fact, they were obviously interested in my water polo and handgun shooting. Perhaps those are the in sports in hot, game-rich countries. Regrettably, rugby was not mentioned. No tradition of that, maybe. I'll see what I can do, though! I do wish things could move quicker. Now that

I have made the decision to go, I would like to be on my way and giving help where I can in some emerging country with urgent needs. I hope that doesn't sound too pi. Will keep you in the picture.

Yours,
Greg Patterson

75

Fairholm
Tabbett Drive
12 September 2005

RD Simms
UN Emergency Force
PO Box 71
Central Africa

My dear Rowena,

Oh, I suddenly feel so much easier in my mind! I had another letter from my neighbour's mother, again asking what I thought of her, the neighbour's, mental state. I had ignored the question – not just as it was asked in her previous letter, but, really, in my own head. Well, this letter compelled me to face up, and I gave the whole business some thought. What's more, I asked my neighbour some rather more pointed, determined questions than I've risked to date.

Anyway, the upshot is that I do sincerely believe now that she is unstable and is imagining the hazards from her husband, poor man. (Yes, he can seem scary, but there is nothing to show one really has anything to be scared about from him.) I asked J straight out why exactly she thought the letter-drop arrangement necessary and she could only answer in the vaguest terms, Ro. She spoke again of the need not to enrage him and said his moods could be frighteningly changeable, but she could not tell me why it would offend him to see her receive letters from her mother. It sounded all very sketchy and pat, as if she were recounting something from a novel. If I were better read I might have recognized it. You like books, Ro, though I don't suppose you have much time for them now. Does her attitude remind you of anything?

And then I asked what I've hinted at before with her – why not telephone? Well, she said she does phone when she can get out to a public booth but that it would be too dangerous to phone her mother from the house or to receive calls there, because of all the extensions and recording things they have. Again, it sounded weak. Almost everyone has these various accessories to their phones these days, and I would have thought her clever enough to deal with all that – neutralize the apparatus temporarily. Or use a mobile, though I know these are not secure. But, of course, the biggest factor in making me think she is sick is her mother's letter. She obviously cannot believe – virtually says this outright – that the husband is as portrayed by her daughter. The mother has already described her daughter to me as imaginative, and it seems pretty clear that the mother thinks the imagination has taken over, run, as it were, riot, regarding the domestic situation. This, from someone whom one would expect to be on her daughter's side, is fairly conclusive, I believe. There is certainly no sign of general battiness in my lady neighbour, but I think, possibly, an intermittent form of persecution mania, and perhaps quite dangerous – because she might feel compelled to defend herself.

I've written to the mother saying something like that, though without using the word mania. She is going to be worried whatever I say, of course. If the husband really is a menace, that's bad. And if it's all in her daughter's unhinged mind, that's bad, too. But I don't think it's serious and I've stressed this. All kinds of people have far-out fantasies in certain aspects of their lives.

Well, it was lovely to come back to the house earlier today and find D alone here, waiting for me. (He has a back-door key.) I know I should not really provide him with one, but it seemed to respectabilize our relationship – as if, for a moment (for as long as Eric's golf game, actually) this were *our* shared home, that's to say, D's and mine, not E's and mine. There's an ancient song: 'You'd Be Nice To Come Home To.' So true! I had just posted off the letter to the mother, and, although I might still have suffered a doubt or two up till then, seeing him here, so attentive and loving, made me certain I had done right. I'd even hung on to the mother's letter, in case I changed my mind about posting mine and needed to consult it again for my reply. But I have destroyed it now – it's not really the sort of thing I want Eric browsing through. He's niggly and suspicious enough already. (I'm laundering a lot more sheets than previously.) I hope there are two people easier in their heads today, the mother and myself. Well, I know I am.

I'll play along for now at least with my lady neighbour's wishes and delusions. They do slur her husband, but no substantive damage is done, I think. Certainly not in the estimation of those who know him well, and I do believe I can claim that now. There are mysterious facets to him, sure, but no man can be interesting without some unknowns, and no woman either. In any case, bluntly to accuse my lady neighbour of lying might do more harm to her shaky mind. From an admittedly selfish, rather grubbily practical, point of view, Ro, it is a good thing that she thinks I accept her version of her husband, because that would make him seem not just unattractive but terrifying. Who would want to run an affair with him?

Sorry this has been all me, but I am a little euphoric, and feel I have emerged from a very dark episode.
Love,
Veronica

76

My dear Marie,

What a lovely way to start the day, your letter arriving this morning. It is sensitive of you to type the name and address on the envelope, which, together with the London postmark, suggests a business communication, fooling her nose. Not that I worry so very much what she thinks, believe me, Marie, but I do like to be the first to open my own letters and not to feel they have been steamed, filleted and resealed by her. Regard it as one of my foibles!

It was the tone of your letter more than anything that gave me the greatest delight, dear Marie. I am so pleased to see that to some degree, anyway, I have been able to convince you that you mean so much to me, that you are not merely some port of call when I happen to be in London for Alain Delon. I feared that to be your view when I last visited London, and I admit I was conscious of a certain coldness. But I feel now from your letter that you know she would never be, will never be, allowed to stand in the way. Certain provisions against that are already in hand, believe me. I greatly look forward to our next meeting in October.

No, I don't think it at all outrageous or coarse that you should have recalled so graphically in your letter some of the intimacies of our recent wonderful days (and nights!) in the capital. Not at all a business letter, in fact! Yes, such beautifully recounted recollections do, indeed, bring warmth and comfort. In fact, I love your frankness, the physicality in words (as well as in actuality!) and fine ability to describe sensation – plus the delicate yet cheerful drawings. The thoroughness of your recollection is matched by my own, and would seem to emphasize the meaningfulness to us both, Marie, of what took place. And, no, no, no, we are, I trust, all adult, and I have absolutely no objection to any of what you call your 'four-letter words', when they are placed accurately in such a happy, loving, almost poetic, context, or as captions to illustrations; though these are so true to life that they scarcely need labelling. In a drab landscape here, such paragraphs and pictures provide the only gleams of excitement, I can tell you.

Ever yours,
Dennis

77

Carthage
Tabbett Drive
Exall DL2 4NG
Monday

My dear Ma,

As luck would have it, I was just now able to watch the terrible street scenes from Iraq on television in the window of an electrics shop while on the way to the General Post Office to make inquiries about poste restante arrangements,

140

in case they should become urgently necessary, owing to Mrs AV Ward and Dennis ardently cahooting. I'm writing this at the post office counter with one of their dodgy pens, so please excuse any untidiness. Also, I shall have to be brief, I fear, owing to the pen being required by members of the public wishing to complete forms etc. Although I could see the Iraq carnage, I could not hear the commentary through the shop window, so was not sure what had happened. In fact, as I stood there, Mother, it struck me that my impression of things symbolized the whole western world attitude. That is, we witness through the media these awful events, but we do not understand, and, even when we think we *do* understand, the whole situation will suddenly change. The dangers faced by many out there would seem to be intense still – troops and civilians – and one is bound to wonder what next, not only in Iraq, but as a pointer to the general worldwide situation. Additional to Iraq, there is continuing tension in Afghanistan, and then what can one say about New Orleans and the draining process? I canot write from the public library reference room at present because of a foolish dispute with the authorities there – foolish on *their* part, let me stress – over what they crudely term my behaviour involving a total misrepresentation by some prudish and possibly voyeuristic assistant, who has allegedly been observing my so-called behaviour for some while – a delightful and educational summer pursuit!

The matter of Mrs AV Ward, OBE (Offer of the Bonk Exceptional), has turned out quite complex. You will have gathered from what I said above that some doubts did persist about whether it's wise to continue to send letters to her lovely home. On the other hand, I also wondered whether suddenly to cease sending them, because she might have developed an understanding with Denn, and this could alert her to my suspicions as to her and him. Obviously, she would realize the letters had their confidential element, or I should not have needed to use her address and then flush the evidence. I have been puzzled, I can tell you, about this whole situation.

Then, out of the blue, I met her by chance in the street. She said she had something sensitive to discuss and could I come back to Fairholm, her lovely house, with her. We sat in the fine room where usually I would read your letters, and once more tea and biscuits were provided. Then came some questions which, to my mind, seemed to suggest that she thought I had a screw loose, if you know that slangy phrase. I could tell she thought I was *imagining*, in fact, fantasizing, the perils of living with Dennis and that they did not really exist. It's all right for her. He sees her probably once or twice a week and that's it – no nasty spells of dangerous cohabitation. I can tell you that I felt like asking her whether her business with Dennis was all in my imagination, also! There is much that is good and recoverable about him, Mummy, if only he could be someone else.

Now and then I find it hard to believe that any woman with an OBE can behave as she does. Yet there have been all sorts with titles, even, who proved unreliable. Think of Lloyd George, an earl! Pleasantly, she said, as though straight out, that she would hate anything to what she called 'throw a blight' upon our mutual neighbourliness. Ha bloody ha, as Cardinal Hume once said. She remarked that you need not put OBE on the envelope if you didn't want to, it being possibly ostentatious. Well, I must have been feeling kindly so I replied it had been well-earned and the least the rest of us could do was acknowledge it.

The weather continues chilly for the season. Whether Mr Blair can continue to hold on in Number 10 is moot. But this is the chance they take when going into politics, plus they all have all sorts of business connections to fall back on if the worst came to the worst.

I must close now in view of the pressure.

Your loving daughter,
Jill

78

Darling Greg,

Didn't I tell you things down there would, as it were, come good again? It would have been desolating and incredible if some spying, triple-initial lout like Nelmes, or whoever, could have put you off your stroke for more than a moment. My view is that Mr JJP Nelmes has now disappeared for keeps, having been rumbled and therefore lost all point. Should he reappear, or anyone in any respect similar, we must obviously take what I would now deem quite justifiable measures against him. The kind of damage he wreaked must never be permitted again.

Dennis has been busy once more churning things out on the bloody word processor in his lair – probably printing off the same stuff over and over for his letters as before, with just the names computer-adjusted, and getting paragraphs, even whole sections, to do three or four letters. The copying and churning out is so easy with a processor, as you know. There are still fine things to dear Dennis, for instance the long periods of absence from my sight, but he remains gravely undigestible, basically.

All my love,
Jill

79

My dear Anna,

What a lovely way to start the day – your letter, just arrived. And yet, of course, it is a grief to hear of the way you are treated in your home. Would that you lived closer, so that I might be of more positive help. The glacial atmosphere you described previously was grim enough, heaven knows, but this is appalling. I do hope you will soon be able to resolve to leave, and as soon as you do, please, please, let me know so that I may be in touch immediately you are back in this country. It will be such a reunion. For myself, things continue as ever, except, of course, that I have taken to observing in person her behaviour away from our home. Although I originally employed a professional for this purpose – and, I believe, quite justifiably in the circumstances – this became unsatisfactory. I think I carry out this admittedly unpleasant and possibly even dangerous work quite as well as he, and there is the advantage that I know these matters now first hand, plus the fact that the unseemliness of her behaviour is not the property of a third party at this stage. If I am ever down on my luck perhaps I could turn private eye! I feel now from your letter that you know she would never be, will never be, allowed to stand in the way. Certain provisions against that are already in hand, believe me.

I love your letters, sometimes with grand sketches included.

In a drab landscape here, such paragraphs and pictures provide the only gleams of excitement, I can tell you. I long to hear you are home – that is, of course, in *this* dear country – and that we are no longer separated by so much damnable geography, dear Anna!

Yours ever,
Dennis

80

Dear Peregrine,

You have ignored my pleas to you and it was only good chance again that enabled me to intercept the note you pushed through the letter box. That note could have created awful trouble here if wrongly found. I am amazed by what you say – that you have been identified and threatened. It is worrying. But I am afraid this cannot change the situation between you and me, Perry. That is over.

J

81

Dear Tim,

Your continuing obsession with Anna is really becoming something of a bore, Tim, if I may say. I do sincerely value your letters, and they have been a true strength to me in my present difficulties. But running through them, and particularly this last, is the suggestion that I am withholding information about Anna from you, and I find this unpleasant, indeed hurtful. May I say, without growing pi, that I fear your interest in her is entirely physical, even lubricious, and it is embarrassing for me to be confronted by your repeated demands to know her whereabouts. Demands which I am quite unable to answer and which, to be frank, Tim, I would not answer if I could. There was a lot more to that girl than merely a rôle as lust object, and I feel the tone of your letter demeans yourself and, more importantly, cheapens Anna, wherever she may be at this juncture.

My own situation, to which you do finally make some grudging reference, remains much as before, I fear, and I build appalling evidence against J, mainly by my own personal efforts now. Of course this is painful to the point of agony. Of course this is degrading. Of course this is possibly hazardous. Simply it has to be done, in the interests of

146

complete veracity. As I pursue these grave, unsettling inquiries, it comes as particularly distasteful, Tim, to be harangued by your ignobly based queries. Further insights into Jill's behaviour have also come my way, but I will certainly not presume to bore you with this now, in view of the obvious fact that your mind is chiefly not upon *my* problems but concerned with reactivating the undignified and provenly dangerous flesh quest which previously caused so much distress, and from which, it appears, you have not learned. No, please do *not* come here. Anna is *not* in this neighbourhood, not even in this country and *not* likely to be as far as I know. I'm afraid I do not believe that any such visit here by you would be 'to offer face to face guidance and support', as you put it, in my continuing agonies. You have caught the whiff of lovely, available womanhood, that's all – or imagine you have.

Your brother,
Dennis

82

Carthage
Tabbett Drive
Exall DL2 4NG
Tuesday

My dear Cindy

Thanks so much for your kind note. I was going to suggest that you'd better write to me care of a neighbour with the OBE, but the situation has grown problematical as she might have become involved with D on a sustained basis. I will try to work out something. I'm afraid you must restrain yourself (selves) for a week or two yet, as, perforce, we shall not be putting on one of our commingling weekends until mid October, owing to various commitments. But it is certainly gratifying to hear that both you and Julian have grown so appreciative. And I know that we and our other guests are likewise appreciative of you and Julian in all your free modes.

The way in which the main parties throw contradictory statistics about the new licensing laws and binge drinking is quite confusing, in my view, but it is obviously the kind of bewildering campaigns we shall have to get used to now MPs are thinking of returning to work. Actually, I do feel quite sorry for all politicians – the way they are described in the various papers as being clueless, sheeplike and weak. Even if true, these are bound to be upsetting remarks for their families, supposing they hadn't noticed those qualities in their loved one. Myself, I sometimes feel Sir Edward Heath had a bad deal and should have been brought back, though more florid late in his life, but without family to be upset by all the abuse.

Your 'words of wisdom' (based on unpleasant personal experience, I wonder, Cindy?!) about the library bit of rough came too late, as you in your practical way might have guessed, I expect. Yes, your words came a trifle late, and certain irritating complications are ensuing therefrom, though not on the health front to date. That would obviously be one of your prime areas of interest, doc!! I've come to agree – been forced to – that bits of rough do tend to treat one as a soft touch in exchange for their devotion and so on. Of course, matching your sharp prediction, I have been given the whole rather laughable thing by him about 'living temporarily with the underclass', for enlargement of the mind, and one's wider social awareness, while awaiting a family fortune. He even referred to George Orwell, an Old Etonian, who went tramping to find what it was like. Role model!

Yet, I certainly do not hold it against people that they should try to live in the imagination. Hardly! Think of the way many psychologists, therapists, etc., prize dreams. There are whole books about the value of fantasy, such as *The Secret Garden*, with some really fruity fantasies as aids to arousal. What's so damn marvellous and superior about reality to a genuine tramp, Cindy, I ask, when shoes cost what they do and you spend most of your time walking? Plus, he is earnestly trying to cut down on cider for his liver and nose veins, so escape through blissful blur by that means is somewhat curtailed.

I have said goodbye to this friend, but, of course, he does not let go so easily, and is hanging about Dennis's and my home and phoning, which can make for niggly problems, as again you rightly forecast. My own feeling, though, as I am sure it would be yours, Cindy, is that people in need like this must be given special consideration, unless and until they grow foully pestilential, which is certainly not quite the case here yet. In that dire case, remedies might be forced on one, regrettably, though what exactly I can't tell. Naturally, I have tried to treat him with full consideration and generosity, poor mendacious mendicant (!) – I knew the way that dopey school taught the distinction between similar words would come in handy one day! Remember how Anthea Middleton kidded the beak she couldn't remember the difference between genial and genital?? But one never knows whether he is actually receiving the communications and benefits I have arranged for him. The Salvation Army hostel is, I am convinced, a wholly fine institution of long-proven worth, but, regrettably, one might not be able to rely on 100 per cent security there.

Dennis, I know, would like to be remembered to both of you and express the hearty wish that we shall see you soon again in our home intermingling and joshing with panache. The weather has turned wonderfully warm again, hasn't it, so that one really does feel glad to be alive.

Warm regards,

Yours,

Jill

83

Dear Greg,

On reflection in rather less excited circumstances, I am inclined to agree with you (*again!*), and there might have been someone there, possibly using a mirror. I don't think the pro snoop is still around but D personally is capable of this, oh yes. Could be something he learned from an Alain Delon film. He really will have to be dealt with, I fear. He cannot be allowed to damage your morale and so on so gravely. Prepare.

J

84

Gregory R Patterson
14A Hill Park
Exall DB7 4SB

Dear Steve,
I'm shortlisted. Pray!
Yours,
Greg

85

*S*ometimes, meeting Jill and Dennis Seagrave, either
together or alone, I get the feeling they have become not
merely, as it were, remote from the life of the Drive and the
district, but are preoccupied with some sort of imagined, yes,
fantasy existence of their own. This might sound presump-
tuous coming from me, comparatively new to the area, but
I've mentioned the I Am A Camera feeling I occasionally get,
and the possible extra insights of a new 'eye'. Anyway, I do
sometimes find it eerie talking to Jill and Dennis. At these
times it's as if they're on a powerfully engrossing hallucino-
genic trip, though I do not mean this literally, and certainly

never suspect them of substance abuse. Rather, they appear committed to thorough, compulsive, complex escapism.

They will chat in the street or shops and for a while react quite normally, yet moments come when they seem to be looking past me, perhaps to some imagined figures or scenes that occupy them far more strongly. Unnerving. Vince has noticed this too. He finds it not just unnerving, but humiliating to be abruptly ignored. He wonders whether they have devised some extraordinary and even dubious make-believe adventures, not just for themselves but possibly involving others, though these others might be unaware of it. All this does remind me a bit of the mysterious, rapt qualities displayed by those two children in Henry James's The Turn of the Screw, *communing with the spirits of people no longer around and whom nobody else can see. Marlon Brando appeared in a poor but chilling film version.*

86

Gregory R Patterson
14A Hill Park
Exall DB7 4SB

HL Sanderson
Head of Games and Leisure Activity
Weald Collegiate

Dear Harry,
   Shortlisted. Fingers crossed.
                Yours,
              Greg Patterson

87

Carthage
Tabbett Drive
Exall DL2 4NG
20 September 2005

Dear Anna,

I'm so lucky! Another letter from you. Oh, yes, she does wonder! A lovely surprise, although it's sad to hear you might not be coming to Britain for what you call 'at least a little while'. Make it as least as possible, dear Anna. No, I still think it would be unwise for you to make contact with Tim, and if you don't mind I will not pass on his address. He has more or less decided to go to ground following that unpleasantness in the past, and perhaps we should respect his wish, Anna.

Affectionately,
D

88

My dear Daughter,

It was lovely to have your newsy letters. All your letters are a welcome tonic, but these did your father and me special good because in several parts of them you seem more settled, and there are quite kindly remarks about Dennis here and there. This seemed so like the Jill and Dennis we like to think of when we consider your marriage. Also there are great good spirits contained in part of your account of socializing.

Don't you think, darling, that this is the *real* Jill and Dennis, and quite different from some of the other pictures you occasionally give in your letters and, indeed, different from parts of this particular letter of yours. I will not specify, but the tone of some of the things you suddenly say in the midst of very pleasant description does strike us as unfortunate, Jill, and, yes, even false. And then we have been thinking over your remarks about a security box in a different bank from the one you and Dennis normally use. Is any security box anywhere, or any letter of disclosure, truly necessary, Jill? We do wonder now and then whether the stresses of life that we all face have forced on you fears not altogether warranted by the facts.

As you say, some of such facts can be seen in two ways.

If Dennis really is reluctant for you to visit us, and would want to be in constant touch while you were here, this could surely mean he values you. Perhaps the possessiveness is a little extreme, but that could indicate the high degree of his affection. This would certainly square with the kindness and thoughtfulness towards you that we always saw in Dennis. Can there *really* have been such an abrupt change?

We do hope you will learn to regard things in a rather more wholesome way, dear Jill, and come to realize that you have a way of life that many, many would envy.

Our best wishes to you and Dennis,
Your loving mother

89

Fairholm
Tabbett Drive
Exall DL2 5NG
21 September 2005

RD Simms
UN Emergency Force
PO Box 71
Central Africa

My dear Rowena,

Well, it's grand to hear you were able to get some relaxation at one of their festival days out there. I sense in your letter that you felt guilty about enjoying yourself and about eating rather more than usual when in a famine country, but it's only once or twice and I think you deserve it.

Myself, I fear I've been guilty (but what the hell?) of some really quite outrageously risky behaviour at social gatherings here – and I mean risky not merely risqué, though it was that, too. Disgraceful and rejuvenating. Frightening and fun. Eric was around and D's wife, of course, so you can imagine the tension. He is *so* audacious. Perhaps I'm becoming audacious, too. An ungovernable pair! Yes, somehow that shared adventure seemed to put me even more firmly into D's camp. Well, no, it's not 'seemed' and 'somehow'. It happened and was inevitable, wasn't it? Anyway, the upshot has been that when he called at the house just now I did agree he could see the latest of his mother-in-law's letters to his wife. I felt it would be not just disloyal to refuse but absurd. Of course, I'm still not totally certain I did right, which is why I'm writing to you again so soon. Sort of confession. Plus, I can plead some extenuating conditions. This time, he asked me more or less direct if I was receiving letters for his wife. It went beyond hints that he knew. The bluntness really helped knock me off balance. And, of course, when I'm off balance I can't think straight – can't think at all. So, this was another reason I admitted it. The point is, when he asked that question, it was really no question at all. He knew the answer. I would have looked so treacherous had I denied it. I could not bear to lose him now and I believe this might have happened if I'd lied.

Also, as I've said, we were here, in the house, while Eric golfed, and – I'm convinced I read this right – D half suggested, or more than half, half suggested, he would break up the drawing room if I did not come clean – and how would I explain that to Eric? D definitely has this ruthless side to him which, of course, is damned intriguing in some ways, but can also be fearsome – and I don't think I take fright easily.

Now and then I get indications from Eric that he suspects. He has begun to talk often about hygiene, in view of the parties that regularly go on at D's house. Mind you, Eric and I are in bodily touch so rarely that he's hardly likely to pick up anything. What worries me, Rowena, is that I could be left with nobody. If Eric turned deeply troublesome and D lost faith in me, where would I be?

It was really some carry-on, as you can imagine, steaming open the most recent letter and then re-sealing it. I remember reading in a spy's memoirs that, despite all the technical advances in espionage equipment, there is still no way to get at someone else's letters secretly, except by the traditional boiling kettle method. I think we did a good, undetectable job, though I realized while crouched over the steam jet in the kitchen, watching the flap peal back, that this was no way for an OBE to behave, whatever folk may think about the Empire these days. But, simply, I felt I owed it to D. He can give me such marvellous excitement and self-belief. This business with the letter and kettle was exciting in itself, and, of course, led to other excitements, from which I'm only just winding down. But I mustn't gloat.

The fact is, this turned out to be pretty much a harmless, good letter, and I can't see any damage was done allowing D to read it. If I felt ashamed I don't think I'd be recounting the episode to you now. Of course, you'll say he'll assume he's entitled to see every letter from now on. I thought of that before I let him have this one. But he does not know when letters arrive here. Now that I have mastered the steaming trick, I can check the letters personally and see whether there is anything that might badly offend him and endanger her in them. If so, he need never know that such a letter has arrived. Censored.

When I describe it as harmless, it was a letter obviously influenced by what I had written to the mother, agreeing that the daughter might well have been over-imagining things, though there was no mention of me, I'm glad to say. The mother's letter suggested this to her, in a very gentle, constructive way, and pointed out that D had always seemed so kind and thoughtful towards her, Jill, in the past. Could there really have been such a violent change? The letter pleased D, and it was almost as if he could sense that its tone owed something to me, though I can't see how he would know.

Anyway, the decision to open the letter seems to have been

justified by the outcome. I will try to help its effects on my lady neighbour by talking to her in the same mildly questioning way about whether there is really a need for secrecy. If she comes to accept this as to the point, there will be no conscience problems about the letters for me, anyway, because they will stop arriving here.

Oh, I know what you're thinking, you cynic. If that happened, would he still be interested in me? I *have* wondered, Ro. But the thought is so terrible I shove it out of the way. One gets used to doing a lot of that as one gets older.

Take care,
Love,
Veronica

90

PEREGRINE AVERS-LANCING IS IT? I BET YOU'VE NEVER HAD SO MANY LETTERS BEFORE AT YOUR FUCKING FLOP HOUSE. I'VE STILL GOT YOU NOTED, SWEETHEART.

91

Mother,

Do *not*, *not*, NOT send any more letters via that fat cow-bitch, Mrs AV Fucking Ward, OBE. She opened the last one. Anybody could see it – the back of the envelope puckered by steam and scruffily resealed. Perhaps *he* read it, too. This would be the only reason he's getting between her tree-trunk legs, to make her show the letters, so he can get between you and me, Ma. I can never allow that. 'Getting between' is his long suit. He'll have to go. Those poor folk in the American South and the storms – first Katrina, now Rita! They sound so harmless, even glamorous, with those female names, like Rita Hayworth, but not at all.

Use the main Post Office poste restante instead. This is really going to give the cow-bitch a massive shock, hopefully up to cardiac arrest pitch, and him, probably, when the letters stop coming to fucking Fairholm.

The crime problems in what a long while ago now we used to call the Soviet Union continue to spread, owing to the dismantling of the secret police and growth of private enterprise. It does make one wonder whether some areas can only achieve stability under a dictatorship. Well, Tito in Yugoslavia was another example. Putin used to be in the secret police himself but retrained for politics under one of their career-change schemes out there.

So, can you see now, Mother, that the situation here is

real and disgusting, not something I've dreamed up, which was what this letter from you in the ruptured envelope suggested. Has someone poisoned you into believing that about me? Does Dennis write to you privately, or that lascivious lumbering cow-bitch, OBE? Of course, he'll be so pleased to read that you think I've gone batty. Already he's been asking me if I feel all right, saying I look pinched and strained. By which he means off my damn head. He'll be thinking that if you say it and then he says it I'll start to believe it, so he can't lose, and maybe I'll really go nuts.

She continued it, too, the cow-bitch, when I went in for this letter. It was all so roundabout and sweet, but she was saying the same thing, really – was I imagining the perils? I felt like an idiot putting the pieces of that letter down her toilet so carefully as ever and double flushing, when knowing that the person I wanted to hide the letter from had probably already seen it. I can just imagine the two sods giggling together while they opened that envelope. They would feel like a real pair of conspirators, a brilliant alliance. I'll get them. Or at least I'll get *him*. Dennis, I know, would wish to be remembered to both of you, and would join me in urging you to keep warm in this rather changeable weather.

Your loving daughter,
Jill

92

Gregory R Patterson
14A Hill Park
Exall DB7 4SB

Dear Steve,

Got it! Working out my notice. Nigeria, here I come. Thanks again for the accolades. I'll be in touch. I think my exit may be just in time. Things are really brewing here now. I have to play along, but, oh, God! A man could get very implicated – and worse.

Yours,
Greg

93

Gregory R Patterson
14A Hill Park
Exall DB7 4SB

HL Sanderson
Head of Games and Leisure Activity
Weald Collegiate

Dear Harry,
   I'm delighted to say I landed one of the posts and am now working out my notice here. I'm feeling really impatient to get away and start some worthwhile endeavour. It's going to be Nigeria. Thanks again for the accolades.
                    Yours,
                    Greg

94

                              Carthage

Dear Greg,
   Just a line to say how wonderful it was last night again

and as ever! And to say how clever of you to obtain the weaponry like that – such firearm contacts in your student gun-club past! I can forgive much, but not what he tried to do, putting his measly self between my mother and me. We can work something out for him now we're equipped. I feel a bit like that woman in *The Postman Always Rings Twice* but I'm not as pretty as Jessica Lange and you're prettier than Jack Nicholson.

Till soon, love,

J

95

Fairholm

Saturday

RD Simms,
UN Emergency Force
PO Box 71
Central Africa

Dear Rowena,

My God, Ro, I think she knows what we did with that letter. No more have come. And my lady neighbour has not been around to see if there's any mail for her. She's usually in here at least every other day. She must have told her mother to write somewhere else. In fact, I have not seen my lady neighbour about at all. I feel sick with shame, and I hate him, hate him now for making me do it. He did make me, Ro. It was not my choice, I pledge. And I hate him, hate him, because now he sees the letter flow has dried, he no longer calls – as you would no doubt have predicted – and as I myself would have in my sharper moments, but I suppressed those. I loathe him so much I'd like to . . . but that's a stupid, violent thought, not suitable for an OBE.

I've been trying to remember what exactly was in that letter from the mother, really going over my recollection of it, in case . . . Well, in case anything in it might have sent him savage. At the time I thought it was a harmless thing, even rather sweet about him, but nobody can tell how he'd react. I worry for her. Oh, Jesus, what a mess I've made.

Write and tell me I'm not a complete shit, Ro – that I might even be able to do something that would make amends to her.

Love,
Alice

96

Dear Peregrine,

Very well, once, *once*, more at the library and you must promise absolutely then not to write here any more or lurk around the house, as you have recently without regard for my safety. I might not be able to make it for a while – possibly a week or two. Things are difficult at home. Very. Simply watch for me, and do not make any kind of approach to this house.

J

97

Carthage
Tabbett Drive
Exall DL2 4NG
4 October 2005

My dear Ma-in-law, or may I call you Gwen!

Jill has asked me to drop you a line because she is not feeling too good – the dreaded flu or similar – and thought you might be worried not to get a letter. I put it all down to the warm summer, helping the bugs to breed! She says to let you know she is basically all right but not quite up to writing letters for a few days. Groggy is her word, and I think that about sums it up. She sleeps a lot, which the doctor says is about the only real treatment (meaning they don't know a thing about it, as usual!). Thus, I would ask you not to phone, as it might disturb her. Many in these parts are going down in the same way. In this regard, I do hope you and Father-in-law are keeping well and looking after your-selves.

My personal wishes for a healthy autumn for you both and I'm sure Jill would wish to repeat hers through me, were she more with it at present. Off to prepare her beef tea now!

Your loving son-in-law,
Dennis

98

Carthage
Tabbett Drive
Exall DL2 4NG
5 October 2005

My dear, dear Marie,

I do not know what to say. The anger in your letter received today could not be more justified. Apologies will probably be of no avail, I do realize that – and regret it so agonizingly. What you say in your letter is, of course, basically true and it would be stupid to attempt denial. I made an idiotic mistake and put my recent letter meant for someone else in your envelope and vice versa. I have to say, yes, there is someone called Anna, and, yes, I did address this Anna here and there with a certain affection, and you are entirely justified in experiencing resentment.

May I say this, though, dear Marie, that Anna is many, many miles away – in South Africa, actually, and married. I know that the letter you received, and which you returned to me with quite warranted abuse written in the margin against her name etc., suggests that she should come back to Britain and that I would be delighted to see her, but believe me this is really only one of those things one has to say to somebody who was once a friend. She is having a bad time and needs such support as she can get, and so one does one's best. I don't believe there is any possibility that she will, in fact, ever return to this country, and, if there were, I would *not* have written in the terms I did, which might then lead

166

to an implied commitment. This was simply to give her something to comfort herself with, a veritable pipe dream.

I feel that this explanation may not altogether allay your
rage, and I would only make one further point, if I may. You
always feared that I might be too closely bound to my situation here, and that you were simply a London diversion. Does
this absurd mistake not prove, dear Marie, that I do need to
look outside, that, because of my domestic dissatisfaction, I
will even conduct clandestine, long-distance correspondence
with a woman I shall probably never see again? Perhaps it is
not only she who draws consolation from this pen pal relationship, if relationship is not too strong a term. (And pen pal
is not right either, I suppose, since I do all my letters by word
processor! Processor-pal doesn't sound quite right, does it?
But whatever we call it, you are so much, much more to me.)
In other words, this girl Anna, far off and not really much
more than a notion to me now, is simply an escape. I do not
even have a picture of her. Writing to her is almost like writing
a piece of fiction, as some do to console themselves and take
flight into the realms of the imagination when life grows too
hard. You, only a couple of hours away by train, are not in
that category at all, believe me. You are someone I think of
as being real flesh and blood – and especially flesh! – part of
my present life, a wonderful part, the most important part, not
some uncorporeal reverie. Darling, there are times when I feel
that, even though you are there and I am here at home, I can
catch the sweet, infinitely thrilling odour of your body. This
is not something that could ever happen with reference to
Anna.

Please believe me, Marie, and let me know that you will
still be there when I come to London soon. No, you are
utterly, utterly wrong to think that I shall now also have to
write to the other woman and try to explain away the letter
with *your* name in it. I do not care enough to do that. It
would bring farce into the situation. She must make what
she will of the error. In a gruesome sense it would, yes, be
comic – I mean as far as she is concerned. As far as you are

concerned it would be tragic if you allowed the mix-up to darken our wonderful relationship.

I think I will have some notable news for you the next time I write, but please let me know I am forgiven first, dear Marie!

Yours adoringly,
Dennis

99

Carthage
Tabbett Drive
Exall DL2 4NG
5 October 2005

My dear Anna,

This is in a sense a gamble, but I think something very terrible may have happened in relation to my recent letter and I am writing now to apologize in advance of your perfectly justified reproaches, should that be. It is a possibly vain attempt to dispel your anger by, as it were, forestalling it. Apologies, though, will probably be of no avail, I do realize that – and regret it so agonizingly. To be blunt, I made a stupid mistake and put my recent letter meant for someone else in your envelope and vice versa.

I have to assume you have received that wrong letter by now and let me admit immediately that, yes, there is someone called Marie, and, yes, I did address this Marie here and there with a certain affection, and you are entirely justified in experiencing resentment.

I feel that this explanation may not altogether allay your rage. I would only make one further point, if I may. I sense that you always feared I might be too closely bound to my situation here, and that you were simply a kind of distant pen pal – an escape (pen pal is not right, I suppose, since I do all my letters by word processor! Processor pal doesn't sound quite right, does it? But whatever we call it, you are so much, much more to me.) Does this appalling mistake not prove, dear Anna, that I do need to look outside – that I have basely to seek fleshly gratification on furtive trips to London because of my dissatisfaction here? In other words, this girl Marie, dear Anna, is not really much more than a sexual consolation for me. I think the coarse terms in which she sometimes writes to me would confirm this, if you saw her letters, owing to their indelicacy, God forbid. You, a long way off, it's true, but the subject of wonderful, vibrant memories, strengthened by sight of the photographs I cherish, are not in that category at all, believe me. You are someone I think of as being potentially a lasting part of my present life, a wonderful part, the most important part, not some dalliance. Darling, there are times when I feel that, even though you are there and I am home, I can catch the sweet, infinitely thrilling odour of your body. This is not something that could ever happen with reference to Marie.

Please believe me, Anna, and let me know that you will still seek me out should you return – and I do hope you will. I know what you must be thinking, but, no, you are utterly, utterly wrong to think that I shall now also have to write to the other woman and try to explain away the letter with *your* name in it. I do not care enough to do that. It would bring farce into the situation. She must make what she will of the error. In a gruesome sense it would, yes, be comic – I mean as far as she is concerned. As far as you are concerned it would be tragic if you allowed the mix-up to darken our wonderful relationship.

I think I will have some notable news for you the next time I write, but please let me know I am forgiven first, dear Anna!

Yours adoringly,
Dennis

169

100

Carthage
Tabbett Drive
Exall DL2 4NG
7 October 2005

My dear Tim,

How delighted we were here to receive your news that Sonia is to have a baby. Jill is abed ill at present – the dreaded flu or similar – but your news was a real tonic for her. I'm sorry you were not able to reach me here by phone, but I have been forced to unplug for considerable periods because of rather bothersome calls from her parents continually asking for bulletins. And because of rather more bothersome calls from someone who puts the receiver down when I answer.

We are already working on possible names for the babe, as I expect you are, too. It is also grand to hear that Sonia thrives as a mother-to-be, and has none of the unpleasant side effects. If it's a he and you call him Dennis be sure it does have the double n, if only to make a difference from the Denis who signed the Dear Bill letters in *Private Eye* – i.e. supposedly Denis Thatcher!

I think, in normal circumstances, it would really have peeved me (again!) to see tacked on to the end of your letter yet another query about Anna. But I can only smile today. Do you really think it is 'proper', Tim, for a father-to-be to be inquiring about an old flame in the persistent way you do? Happily – from my point of view, anyway – I still have no knowledge of her whereabouts and so can honestly and relievedly say I'm unable to help, and advise you, dear father-to-be and brother, to get back to the responsibilities of approaching parenthood.

Once more, then, warmest congrats from us both and tell Sonia to look after herself.

Your brother, now due to be a proud uncle,
Dennis

101

Carthage
Tabbett Drive
Exall DL2 4NG
12 October 2005

Dear Sir,

I know your name is Gregory, but far be it from me to address you so. I have reason to believe you telephone this property from time to time, pretending to be a salesman of some sort or rudely cutting the call when I reply. I have certain information on you, which has been professionally acquired and which enables me to write to you now, with your full name and address. I also have reason to believe that when you telephone here it is because you are seeking my wife. I write to say she will have no more truck with you and it could not be more impossible for you to speak with her or see her.

Yours faithfully,
DW Seagrave

102

STILL KEEPING TABS ON YOU, PERRY BOY.

103

Carthage
Tabbett Drive
Exall DL2 4NG
Friday

Dear Anna,

You choose not to accept my apology, which is entirely your right, of course, but your express letter amazes me. I made a simple stationery error and because of that you harp back to long buried turmoils in our lives and scream about what you call 'parallel duplicities' to that time. It's a fine phrase, but I reject it. A woman who started out as your dear friend became, in your view, your worst enemy because, also in your view, she had begun to take precedence over you in the regard of my brother and myself. Was not that woman eventually removed from our lives as a means of placating you, Anna, and in circumstances which still freeze my soul when I recall them? For you to see

similarities between that situation and my harmless friendship with Marie in London, based utterly and exclusively
on common filmic interests, is absurd. I'm afraid I detect
threat in your letter. Yes, of course I know you live in a
violent country and I understand what you say when you
tell me you have learned how to 'deal with people, point
blank if necessary'. For all that picturesque talk, I shall
still be delighted to see you in this country, dear Anna, and
I'm delighted to hear that at last you are actually coming.
Please do get in touch.

Yours,
Dennis

104

Carthage
Tabbett Drive
Exall DL2 4NG
Saturday

Dear Marie,
   You choose not to accept my apology, which is entirely
your right, of course, and I will accept your decision that
things are at an end. But was it necessary, sweetheart, to
talk like that – the reference to 'certain heavy friends'.
What does this mean? All I did was make a simple stationery
mistake, for heaven's sake. Let us at least remain on civilised
terms, and not have recourse to picturesque hints and threats.
Please do not try to contact me here again, though.

Yours,
Dennis

173

105

Carthage
Tabbett Drive
Exall DL2 4NG
17 October 2005

Dear In-laws,

Jill, I'm afraid, is still rather under the weather and has asked me to drop another line. It's this nasty thing that is going the rounds and which, while not dangerous, saps the energy over a long period and makes everything such an effort. She is still sleeping a great deal, which would probably explain why you were unable to get an answer by telephone. I, of course, am still out quite a bit, my business demands being at full pace.

Jill insists that you should not worry and the both of us would like to repeat our urgings to you to beware chills in this changeable season and, if at all possible, to keep away from places where infection is likely: public transport, cinemas, supermarkets, pubs, restaurants. She feels that, on this account, despite your kind offer, it would be most unwise of you to risk coming here, much as we long to see you, of course, and I'm afraid I have to agree with her on this at present.

Your ever loving son-in-law,
Dennis

106

Carthage
Tabbett Drive
Exall DL2 4NG
25 October 2005

My dear Marie,

Of course I don't despise you for ignoring my orders –
so harsh and pompous that makes me sound, but quite justifiably, I fear – not to contact me again – absolutely the
reverse! Such things are written in the pain of the moment,
really only a childish snarl of protest against rejection. I'm
sorry you were not able to reach me here by phone 'to
make it right with a nice talk', as you so happily and
constructively put it, dear Marie, but I have been forced to
unplug for considerable periods. This is because of rather
bothersome calls from Jill's parents and more than bothersome calls from, I'm afraid, one of her brazen admirers,
a Volvo owner called Greg, which I've ascertained from
certain inquiries – though he is never brazen enough to
come clean and say he is who he is, when I answer. If there
is one thing I loathe it is that kind of shiftiness, not because
it involves Jill, I might say, but because it is so craven and
so rude.

You are a sweetheart to risk your pride by writing to me
again, and to say so generously that you can understand my
anger in that previous dark letter – and can even see that the
coldness in it all sprang from the agony I went through, and
had absolutely no basis in my real feelings. You mean so

175

much to me. Your mind. Your caring personality and humour. You mean everything. I think you know this. I hope so.

It is great to hear that you will be waiting for me when I arrive for the Alain Delon researches. I long for the day, and nights.

With all my love,
Dennis

107

Tabbett Drive

My dear Anna

What a delight to receive your further express letter. Certainly, certainly, we shall 'let bygones be bygones', and it is lovely of you to be so forgiving, though wonderfully typical.

I'm sorry you were not able to reach me here by phone but I've been forced to unplug for considerable periods because of rather bothersome calls from Jill's parents, and more than bothersome calls from, I'm afraid, one of her brazen admirers, a Volvo owner called Greg, which I've ascertained from certain inquiries – though he is never brazen enough to come clean and say who he is when I answer. If there is one thing I loathe it is that kind of shiftiness, not because it involves Jill, I might say, but because it is so craven and rude.

You are a sweetheart to risk your pride by writing to me again. Although you are still at such a distance, dear Anna, I feel myself to be very much in touch with so many aspects of you. Your mind. Your caring personality and humour. You mean everything. I think you know this. I hope so.

It is great to hear that you might – I say no more than might! – be coming this way before much longer. I will be waiting.

With all my love,
Dennis

108

Carthage
Tabbett Drive
Exall DL2 4NG
28 October 2005

Dear Timmy,

How strange that I should revert to addressing you like that after all these years! I suppose this pleasant echo of childhood has been brought on by the prospect – admittedly distant at this date – of a little one joining your family. It's this prospect which causes us to advise, Tim, that it would not be wise for you to visit here just now as you propose. Jill remains somewhat under the weather and fears she may yet be infectious. Also, she is still a little low after it all – the dreaded flu, or similar, of course – and not quite up to the hostess rôle at the moment, though both of us do appreciate your excitement about the baby and your wish to share your happiness face to face.

What would be nice, we thought, is if, when the baby is here, the four of us could meet up at some halfway point for one of those weekend breaks in an hotel. This would allow everyone a relaxing time and give us the much anticipated delight of making the acquaintance of this new and, I'm sure, beautiful Seagrave.

Things continue here in their own sweet way, but for Jill's illness, which is now, fortunately, on the wane. We both send you and Sonia our very best, but no virulent bugs, I hope!
Your brother,
Denn

109

27 Perdita Close
Amberchase
Lancs
28 October 2005

Dear Mrs AV Ward,

I'm going to be frank and say that Jill told us not to be in touch with you ever again, but we are desperate, and I cannot believe that someone with a decoration, which I know you hold, would behave deceitfully. We have had nothing from Jill for some time and are unable to reach her by telephone. We are so anxious that we would travel to see her now, despite her strict word against that, but my husband is not too well at present. We are told the same about Jill by *her* husband, when we are able to get a reply on their telephone – i.e. that she is not well. We wonder why she never answers the telephone, even though they have so many extensions there, including one, surely, in a sick room.

I do not know how you will use this letter, nor whom you will inform of its contents. I do not care very much. But, Mrs Ward, could you please, please, do what you can to discover whether Jill is all right? Perhaps you've seen her in the street lately?

This would be enough to put our minds at rest, and surely nobody could blame you for giving us such a harmless piece of information – harmless, yet to us, I assure you, immensely valuable and comforting.

Yours,
Gwen Day (Mrs)

110

Fairholm
Tabbett Drive
Exall DL2 5NG
3 November 2005

Dear Mrs Day,

Your letter moved me. I do not know why Jill should have told you to avoid contact with me here, and I regret it greatly. However, this certainly does not prevent me from having her interests still very much at heart, and yours also. I will certainly do what I can to confirm she is all right. I haven't seen her about lately, it's true, and, as a matter of fact, had assumed she was visiting you. But there is a lot of seasonal sickness around and I'm sure you would have heard from her husband if there were anything to worry about. I will write when I have discovered something.

Yours sincerely,
Alice Ward

111

LISTEN MR PEREGRINE AVERS-FUCKING-LANCING, HAVEN'T YOU LEARNED YET THERE IS NO POINT RINGING HERE? SHE IS NEVER GOING TO ANSWER. I KNOW IT'S YOU, YOU BASTARD, EVEN THOUGH YOU CUT THE PAYPHONE CALL WHEN I SPEAK. I'LL BE LOOKING FOR YOU.

112

Fairholm
Tabbett Drive
Exall DL2 5NG
4 November 2005

RD Simms
UN Emergency Force
PO Box 71
Central Africa

Dear Rowena,
Things get worse, sis, and I still need a shoulder to cry on, I fear. It seems preposterous that *I* should be writing to

you for comfort, when you have such terrible things to face there. But I'll keep it short.

As you suggested in your latest phone call, I would let it all die now, if I could, and settle down to a life of eternal drabness with Eric and my OBE. But the neighbour's mother has written, despite the steaming – which she obviously knows about – and has asked me to find out what has happened to her daughter. Well, I wondered myself, of course – that guilty feeling I think I've already bored you with. Anyway, I keep my eyes open, in case I see her, but don't. I *do* see him, though, coming and going, but never coming and going to/from here any more. Eric would become enraged if he saw me go to their house, because of what allegedly takes place there some weekends, so I had to try to catch D in the street by watching from the window until the right moment.

Eventually, I did manage it and asked about his wife. He said she was ill, a really bad bout of flu which had laid her out for weeks. It's possible, I know. I'll write and tell the mother what he says, but, of course, it's no more than she's already heard, and from the same source, which she doesn't trust. Do I? I don't know, Rowena. What hurt me so much about this conversation with him was that it damn well entirely concerned his wife. He gave not the slightest sign there had been a relationship between him and me – just polite, blank, street talk. I detest him.

Well, I feel better for that. Thanks for listening again. Tell me all *your* woes next time you write or phone. But you never seem to have any!

Love,
Alice

113

Jilly, where are you? You said a week or two at the you know where. Sorry, but I've got to write because it's always him answers the phone . . .

P

114

Carthage

Peregrine,
  I've been ill. Tomorrow night there.

J

115

Carthage
Tabbett Drive
Exall DL2 4NG

My dearest Mother,

Happily fully restored after an encounter with Mr Flu in person, I am writing immediately to let you know I'm fine. Apologies for the long silence. I hope you weren't anxious.

In fact, the weather here has not become truly wintry yet – more like the tail end of a benign autumn, and I'm sorry to have missed so much of it while laid up. I feel, also, I've lost track of the news, owing to a bad lack of interest while feverish and snotty. I don't know what the situation is in Iraq or Palestine, also the eternal nattering about the Conservative leadership is only half intelligible to me. I'll have to postpone discussion of these topics till my next, when I hope to have caught up.

Obviously, I must put off for a while my visit to you as I am still quite weak, and he would be concerned over my travelling solo in that condition. It would be quite all right, though, for you and Dad to come here some time in the future, if you could face the journey. In fact it would be wonderful! All traces of infection should have packed up and well and truly departed by then, I feel sure, and you would not be at risk from that especially vile bug. Please let me know your views. I do not think the visit should be immediate, but definitely in due course.

I shall not write much today, having to catch up on letters

to quite a few folk who might wonder where I have been this last I-don't-know-how-long! I just want to let everyone know I am OK, and naturally I am writing to you and Dad first, though, inevitably, there is little to say, having been out of things for such a while.

Dennis, I am sure, would wish me to convey his warmest, and would add his own sincere endorsement to my invitation to visit us.

Your loving daughter,
Jill

116

Carthage
Tabbett Drive
Exall DL2 4NG
4 November 2005

Darling Greg,
Things have been slightly fractious here making it *difficult* to get in touch. It's not altogether resolved yet and I have to ask you, I fear, to be patient a little while longer. You *are* still out there, aren't you? I might be able to make it to our Portakabin spot soonish. Will let you know.

Lovingly,
Your Jill

117

Carthage
Tabbett Drive
Exall DL2 4NG
6 November 2005

My dear Cindy,

You are the only one I can tell about the following, for reasons which I am sure you will soon see. I do need to tell *someone* and my feeling is that, owing to matters witnessed and fully participated in by you during weekend gatherings here, Cindy, I can safely disclose what follows to you. Please, please destroy this letter immediately, and if down a toilet ensure all fragments are minute and are carried away, particularly if the toilet is in your hospital and available for general use, and thus to prying eyes should particles remain floating, with certain words standing out at no great distance from users. Preferably destroy this in an incinerator, common in hospitals and more final.

An evening, a week or so ago, he made it clear that he knew about the acquaintance from the library reading room, Peregrine, whom I have mentioned to you; a vagrant in many respects, yet young and in considerable, pitiful need, not just materially but generally. As I told you, I have tried to break this relationship, but agreed to one last meeting. D has, I think, been following me in that little way of his, and may have observed certain friendly contacts between Peregrine and myself. I believe, also, he knows about another acquaintance of mine, but it was Peregrine who preoccupied him on the violent evening I feel I must tell you about now. Obsessed, rather than preoccupied, would be a better word for Denn's condition. Perhaps I should not write all this down, which is why I ask that you destroy this letter immediately. My own impression is that he thought there was some disgrace in his wife – *his* wife – being in physical contact with someone who is a vagrant pro tem. It is possibly the health aspect of relations with a sleep-anywhere tramp, as you in your métier would understand, Denn being quite the hypochondriac, the poor fusspot thing. He would be scared of someone like the other interesting acquaintance of mine, whom I am sure he also knows of, and who has a Volvo and so on – i.e. possesses status and some class. But a vagrant is to Dennis a different kettle of fish, someone easier to deal with, someone suitably weak and at risk, as well as possibly contaminated by not just unsafe sex but unkempt sex here and there.

Naturally, denying in the first instance that I had any kind of close association with Peregrine, I had to ask Dennis strenuously, and with conviction, did he really think it likely in the least that I would take up with someone who, according to his description, was an obvious hobo or pikey, me coming from this kind of fine house and select district? He kept on and on, and, because of a sudden turn to extreme brutalities, I have not been able to go out, and he has stayed home and made sure I do not write or receive calls, in that little way of his. My hand was somewhat damaged again, through trying to protect myself, so that writing became difficult, and forgive me, do, if it's still a trifle wobbly, especially as I'll have to go on a bit in this letter, the hellish details being important. I fear that, owing to the silence, my parents may think something terrible has happened, which they are prevented from discovering. And possibly my other friend has been unable to make contact, either. It is impossible to reach him by phone because of some cow-bitch on reception at his office, and I get no returned calls from his answer service at home or voice mail. A runner? In any case, it is very dangerous to phone from here because of various snoop devices, which I've mentioned previously.

This is the first chance I've had to write anything, though he is still around the house somewhere and I'm listening carefully in case he comes padding near on the beige fitted carpet. I'll try to write to Mother and Father also today despite the long time spent on this letter, though posting will be a difficulty.

I had to eventually admit, owing to pressure, that I knew Peregrine, and horrifically, Cindy, Dennis said to me – and this without rage and quite coolly – that he had considered slaughtering me on account of the degradation and contamination my relationship with Peregine brought him. No surprise, because I, too, had feared this to be his intention during the violence I received involving a tyre lever. But he remarked that he had decided instead to finish off 'stinking' Peregrine – which was his term, Peregrine being a vagrant in many respects, and therefore in his view unsavoury – and he would kill him for 'polluting' me and consequently our marriage, and that nobody was going to do much about looking for the killer of a tramp.

Cindy, I expect you can can imagine how this appalling statement shocked me, and I cried out in disbelieving and heartfelt protest, but he would not listen. At times Dennis can be so resolute and bold, something you would not expect usually from such a half-baked, topiarizing fart. Needless to say, despite fears for lovely Peregrine, there was clearly something exciting in what Dennis proposed, and I did see marked evidence of him really caring for me, in his particular way. He said he wouldn't use the tyre lever this time because this would mean a kind of additional bond between Peregrine and me, both having been attacked with it. Saying I had to be a willing party to what would happen, he insisted I should accompany him on this purging mission, as he termed it. You can imagine that this idea went immensely against the grain in view of my high affection for Peregrine, despite the clothes and all that shit about a delayed inheritance, but on balance and after terrible heart-searching I thought I'd better attend, there appearing to be some chance I might be able to save him somehow. He said to wear a scarf around my face, not just to conceal the marks there but for general anonymity. Even if I had not gone, it would have made no difference and I knew this. Please, please, don't think of me as cold, except the deadly coldness of abiding horror at what he suggested.

You being a doctor, dear Cindy, will know well, probably, how much the human body can stand and still retain life, even a human body not at all well nourished, and abused by habitual rough cider, as in Perry's dear case. It was easy to find Peregrine because

Sorry! I had to break off there because I heard him approaching slitheringly from upstairs and it was necessary to push these sheets of paper behind a picture of Marco Polo hanging on the wall. Exploring appeals to Dennis, as if he'd ever be capable of anything like that. But they do say now that Marco Polo never even went to China, and he could not have discovered it. So if the sheets of this letter are a bit smudged and crumpled, imagine it's been run down by a horde of Chinese horsemen! Or maybe not!

Resuming, however, it was easy to find Perry because, although banned from the library reading room owing to various incidents, he still hangs around that part of the town, the little gardens there and the patio, with certain unsavoury piss-artist colleagues, Heavy Royston and Bert Westra, swigging, begging, abusing passers-by, as is their traditional métier. Obviously, even with the scarf in place, it was necessary for me to stay well back, for he would recognize me regardless, despite it being at night. Obviously, Dennis wanted Peregrine on his own. He grew enraged because of the presence of the tramp colleagues. But, fortunately, when it grew late, Royston and Bert seemed to decide they would sleep in a doorway at the rear of M&S, which is a good, deep doorway, not generally too unsavoury, and usually with some waste packing paper stacked there, which the poor blighted ones can use for bedding. This is a spot I have heard Peregrine speak well of previously, known as a fold, as in the hymn: 'Ninety and nine that safely lay in the shelter of the fold.' In any case, these two were too pissed to walk to the Salvation Army hostel, but Peregrine has been really cutting down, the good lad, and could easily manage this journey to the hostel, where I believe he is well thought of and where they turn a blind eye to his coming in late.

I don't know if you are familiar with this area where the hostel stands, but approaching it on foot from the town you can take a short cut over a big redevelopment site and, of course, this was horribly opportune for Dennis, myself staying back still. What he had brought with him is what is known as a Stanley knife, which is a perfectly legal and valid knife for all kinds of domestic and professional tasks such as carpet laying, but deadly when put to ill use. It really astonished me to see how proficiently Dennis could use the knife in this context, it bearing no resemblance to topiary work – although he did have army training, of course, which he claims was SAS. He would, wouldn't he? My heart went out to dear Peregrine, obviously, with many happy memories, moving forward carefully in his rather slow way over the rubble, although he was only squiffy rather than completely rat-arsed, and at one point I could not prevent myself from crying out to warn him before the first blow, my longing to save him still intense. I know now this was a mistake, for it caused him to turn. Perhaps he recognized my voice, perhaps he recognized me, though I was in the shadows, against some office block they're putting up, yet another unlovely cement brick tower. So, ironically, when he turned, it was easier for Dennis. He had that Stanley knife into the side of Peregrine's neck twice in no time, really arcing blows with fierce strength. You would not think the half-baked, privet poltroon had it in him, like some released metal spring. So perhaps he really was SAS.

Particular details of that scene stay in the head, Cindy, and I have to write them down to rid myself of them. Stacks of grey-black breeze blocks bound with wide plastic strips like parcels. A vandal-ruined Portakabin rendered window-less and with its door hanging on one hinge. The underfoot rubble and mud, the mud reddish brown, a filthy morass after rain. Though not totally drunk, Peregrine was not great on his feet and went down backwards on to the ponytail, adored by me, into this reddish brown morass. He, too, gave a cry, perhaps just pain, perhaps directed at me if he knew I was there? A terrible farewell, and for the first time ever I wondered if he really did come from a fine family because this cry sounded quite cultured, not a base, craven scream but more like a noble protest at this crude, bloody affront, as a warrior king in history might have protested at an attack by a mere trooper.

Bending, Dennis struck at him again and again, neck, throat, body, through those poor clothes and the fun waist-coat. Even from where I stood, I could see from the neck a sudden great spout of blood, like a sperm whale. With the blood, Dennis was struck in the face and about the shoulders and copiously. He did not draw back. This, as you would know, Cindy, must have been jugular blood, and quite a final matter. Peregrine, the dear, made no more sound, as if enough had been said, which again gave an impression of nobility. Raising his head, Dennis beckoned to me hard and masterful with his free hand, wanting me to come and see, in order to prove his point that this source of 'pollution' had been removed. Also, he said he wanted me to check he was dead. This is not my area, as it is yours, Cindy, but I did not want to prolong the event, especially with Dennis looking like that, and said, weeping badly, 'Yes Perry is dead.' But then Perry moved in that rubble and morass, not much, but a movement of one of his poor legs in the hopeless, penguin-suit trousers. Dennis went at him again. To me, it was a surprise he could see properly, this coat of blood over his face, his eye lashes clogged. In the end, Perry stopped moving, no question.

Strangely, upon return, Cindy, he having put his clothes ready for disposal by fire in the morning, and washed the

Stanley knife, we had to make love till dawn, owing to adrenaline. Have you seen *The Postman Always Rings Twice*, when Jack Nicholson and Jessica Lange similarly need to get passionate with each other in the open air after killing her hubbie? Like that. Life does go on, as you will be aware. Our juices are strange forces, as you will also be aware, both from a doctor's and woman's point of view. (This is what I mean when I say please ensure that this missive is properly destroyed. Even parts of it could give understandable offence.)

We look forward to seeing you and Julian soon, both of us great fans of your warmth and friendliness and Julian's ready, yet unclumsy, wit.

Your friend,
Jill

118

Well, the Seagraves are still with us, and the cormorant and the bison, gloriously completed, look now like proud and eternal denizens of the Drive. In some senses the Seagraves could be described as that themselves, of course, in contrast to our jumped-up selves. Encountered in the street recently, Dennis said his object with the two creatures was to give an international flavour to Carthage, by depicting a bird native to our country and an animal which is foreign. I replied that Tabbett Drive in general benefited from the range implicit in his work and he said he hoped so, indeed. This sounded very much like commitment. I see his efforts as not simply topiary but topiary with a mission. This is a part of what the Drive would lose should the Seagraves depart.

So, thank God, they seem settled – which helps me, and yes, Vince, to feel settled, also. In fact, I have come to think lately that Vince would be even more upset than myself if the Seagraves did up and go. I can't work out exactly what makes me sense this, but the impression is strong and insistent. Perhaps he has come to feel, as I do, that there is a sort of symbolic quality to the Seagraves, and a symbolic quality which is deeply helpful to us. They represent continuity, yet not a continuity which has been easily or simply achieved. One does occasionally suspect there might have been some kind of temporary, deep dissatisfaction with Tabbett Drive in their household. Possibly, having been here a while, and married a while longer, they felt defeated by the decent ordinariness and calm of the Drive. These are qualities I, personally, prize, but, then, Vince and I are only fairly recently wed, and are newcomers to the district. We haven't really had time to grow bored, with the Drive or with each other. I hope the Seagraves have decided they should buckle down to things as they are rather than indulge in unrealistic and uncomfortable restlessness. And I can, I think, now believe it is so. I say this with some hesitation, some tentativeness, but, yes, I do believe it.

119

Carthage

My dear Mother,
   Just a brief note, because of shock, to say that a friend of mine from the public library who was due to inherit

lands and various properties in due course has been found stabbed to death on wasteland. I might have mentioned him previously. The people of Iraq, I suppose, would hardly notice such a single death, but to me it is quite a considerable upset. He had faults, yes, but not overwhelmingly so. He was, in fact, the sort of man who had many friends, not all of them entirely law abiding, I fear, and it seems to me that they might well be looking for revenge for this brutality on a colleague. They would not trust the police, I fear. Oh, but violence is everywhere in this modern society.

Dennis, I know, would wish me to send you his very best wishes, and I do also, of course.

Your loving daughter,
Jill

120

Fairholm

Dear Ro,

Something terrible is happening to this town. First a tramp slaughtered in a frenzied attack and now my neighbour, D, found dead – murdered, shot on a building site. Rumours, whispers, that D's death could be some kind of revenge killing for the tramp? I do not understand. Will write in detail when I feel more settled.

Yrs,
Alice

121

Carthage
14 November 2005

My dear Mother,

A note to say thank you so much for making that long journey to Dennis's funeral and for the lovely flowers. Well, bleak Mr Winter seems to be really on the way now and the birds have left for sunnier climes – at least the sensible ones have! Not that our winters are usually all that bad. My own view is that we are extremely fortunate to live in such a temperate climate, and I have little sympathy with those who are always complaining about our weather.

Police have been here a lot, obviously, questioning, hinting. I am going to try to keep up Dennis's hedge figures personally. It will feel strange to be on his personal stepladder. The police discuss his business and his life generally, trying to discover motives and enemies. They're cagey, but they seem to be saying there was something pretty dark in the past involving Dennis, Tim, a girl called Anna and another girl, and they wonder if this death is tied to it somehow. Apparently, they've traced this Anna and, interestingly, she's in Britain from South Africa.

The Liberal Democrats are still bound to be a mystery element in all the predictions about future politics, particularly in view of the Conservatives' continual problems.

I'd always guessed there was something unpleasant to this Anna, but I'm not any clearer. The weekend things will have to go into suspension for a while, I think, out of respect.

I was so pleased to be able to introduce you to Mrs AV

Ward, OBE, and her hubbie at D's funeral. She put a good face on things, the bold old slag, but you will have noticed did not have the nerve to come back here afterwards for sherry and sandwiches. Police will nose around Dennis's London contacts, too, looking for those who might have a reason to hate, plus any local connections. I feel rather odd being linked in some way with two people slaughtered here, never in the past having been associated with anyone murdered at all. Do keep warm and well. I shall be able to think of a visit to you soon, now dear Dennis is no longer here to fret so touchingly over my absence.

Your loving daughter,
Jill

122

Fairholm

My dear Rowena,

I can still hardly talk or write about these terrible things, so excuse any shapelessness to this letter. Apparently, the assumption is D might have been tailing someone (his wife?) to a notorious site for lovers.

Police and press have been everywhere. I know several of the officers through my job at the Police Authority, but it doesn't help. I say what people always say at these times, that the Seagraves were on the whole quiet neighbours who kept themselves to themselves, yet were never stand-offish. Eric's been chirping a different song, naturally, and I don't know whether the contrast will make for trouble.

The funeral was hellish. My neighbour did introduce me

to her parents and they were all civil, but I had the impression she felt I was responsible for the death. I couldn't decide whether she minded.

Our local paper came out with a headline something like: 'Was Murdered Man A Peeping Tom?' Oh God, Ro, isn't it awful? The report said in that horribly blunt way of the press that the thirty-five-year-old insurance broker found shot dead on a building site might have been trying to spy on lovers. According to the paper, the spot, near the main public library, is often used by couples. Vandalized Portakabins provide shelter, and D's's body lay close to one of these cabins.

Detectives believe he might have been voyeuring sex activities and was discovered and killed by an angry beau. He had been shot once in the head. Of course, the police are keen to contact people who were at the site on Tuesday night, but are not getting much cooperation, despite appeals via the media. Who'd want to admit publicly they were at such a dubious spot, even if there had been no murder? The journalists had been to see Jill Seagrave. Their report said she was still in shock, but came briefly to the door of what they called, in their predictable jargon, 'her detached, executive-style home', and told them she had no idea why Dennis would be on a building site late at night, although he worked irregular hours and was often out in the evenings visiting clients.

And then more jargon about the Drive – 'select' and 'tree-lined', that kind of envy-filled nonsense – and paragraphs of neighbours' views of the Seagraves: a very loving pair and so on, who generally lived a quiet life but occasionally threw large weekend parties to which nobody in the Drive was invited. Somebody referred to these as 'a mystery'. The police will not say whether they think there is a connection between the two murders – the vagrant's and D's – both near the public library.

Forgive me, Ro, but I can't write any more about this situation. It sickens and depresses me too much.

All my love,

A

123

Bastard, bastard, bastard, Greg.

I'm sending this via your ex-office here, sure they have a forwarding address for you in Africa, you slime. I almost hope they will open this, so they will know what a piece of yellow muck you are. After all that talk, you disappear and leave me to do it solo. Which I did. Which I did. Which I fucking did.

Maybe even where you are hiding you hear of such things as a snooping, skulking, voyeur's death, you cringing, scarpering piece of gutlessness. Nigeria, they said when I rang your office – that tart on reception. She will not cough anymore. Are you keeping in touch with her? You must have been planning this escape all the time we were talking of our project. I felt sure the Portakabin area would suit. And I also felt sure he would tail me again. But you? Where were you? Oh, Greg.

This will be unsigned and from no address. But you'll know who's writing. Don't consider doing any public duty talking about it. Remember who supplied the item that did the damage, won't you? And remember your name is on those snoop papers. Much motive, it would seem to them, laddy. OK, much motive it would seem to them for me, too.

Naturally, I removed those reports from their hiding place in the filing cabinet. This place has been swarming with cops. But the reports are not destroyed, dear one, just banked in my private deposit box. They would spotlight you, no matter where you're cowering and slinking. I've had a quantity of shitty, rough questioning, as you might imagine – but could you care less? Anyway, so far so good, and who can say better than that?

It doesn't look as if the author of the snoop reports and his bosses have disclosed anything to the police. Perhaps they're like priests and doctors, sworn to secrecy.

But how could you do it, Greg – bolt like that? Didn't any of it mean a thing to you – the joy of it, the fun ... well, the love? Oh, darling Greg, I'm desolate. You'll come back? Please! Everything's so easy now, as we planned. I can take phone calls at home. Call? Do they have phones out there?

Love ... yes, regardless

124

Carthage

Dear Cindy,

Thank you so much for your lovely letter of sympathy over the loss of Dennis and for the fine wreath from you and Julian. Yes, it would be lovely to resume our friendship and fine get-togethers once grief has somewhat abated. I feel very lonely. I have suffered one terrible loss, and on top of this comes Dennis's death in Portakabin environs. But at least the weather is kindly for the moment. My own view is that we are extremely fortunate to live in such a temperate climate, and I have little sympathy with those who continually complain.

Very best wishes to you and Julian,
Jill

125

Dear Mrs Seagrave,

Perhaps the name JJP Nelmes will be strange to you among all the letters of sympathy received, but I am writing formally to express my deep condolences upon the death of your husband, which I read of in the press. If I might at this point strike a relevant note, I had a professional relationship with your husband of which you might not be aware. Or then again, you might. Your late husband terminated this relationship some time ago, but I had become interested in the matter on what might be termed a personal basis. As a result, I was able to establish what might be regarded as a significant fact concerning a former acquaintance of yours, Mr Gregory R Patterson. This was to do with the purchase and supply of an item that might well have a bearing on things as they so tragically turned out in the Portakabin area. Unfortunately, this information was not available until long after Mr Seagrave terminated the contract, and therefore it did not appear in certain reports that I furnished, and of which you may not be aware – or possibly you may. However, the information was subsequently confirmed to my professional satisfaction. Your husband decided he could carry out the work that I had been originally engaged for, and it might well be that he met his death while so doing.

It has occurred to me, Mrs Seagrave, that you would

possibly wish to, as it were, resume the discontinued contract in the place of your late husband. This would be particularly in respect of my discoveries as to Gregory R Patterson and said purchase, etc. Owing to the termination of the contract with the firm of Lavery, this resumption would be with me independently, as signed below, and not with the company. The essence of this understanding between us, Mrs Seagrave, would, of course, be total confidentiality, which I'm afraid I could guarantee only if we are in a contractual state. My anxiety is that, if this matter were known, or became known, somehow to the police, it might change the direction of their inquiries which, I understand, are at present focussed towards a possible London connection, or possible former South African connection.

There will be a, what we term, nominal, one-off, up-front consideration or fee to ratify this re-activated contract, namely £30,000 (thirty thousand pounds), obviously to be paid in cash. I have no doubt your husband was well-insured, being in the business.

Now that the proper formality of a condolence letter has been fulfilled, I shall be in touch by telephone, if I may, to say how and where this consideration may be delivered. May I express once more my own, my colleagues' and my family's feelings for you at this time of sadness, no doubt intensified by the abject and hurried withdrawal of Mr Patterson to Nigeria before matters grew irreversibly dodgy for him.

Yours sincerely,
JJP Nelmes

126

Fuck you, Nelmsey, but OK. Where in Nigeria?
JS

127

Carthage
Tabbett Drive
Exall DL2 4NG
2 December 2005

Dear Anna,
  Going through Dennis's things I came across some letters
from you, one of which must have arrived on the day of his
rather unfortunate death. It is lovely to know you are back
in Britain, and I'm sure Dennis would have been delighted
to reply to this recent letter in person had he only lived. I
expect you read of the mysterious 'Portakabin shooting' in
the press. It seems a century since you and I met. This part
of the year is one of the most trying, I feel – the short days
and diabolical winds – but we should not complain, should

we, not when we recall what happened in New Orleans? I heard the police wanted to talk to you about Dennis's death, wondering whether you sent thugs to do him in on account of some sexual conflict. This seems a very worrying way of being welcomed back into this country for you! I know you will be relieved to hear that all the rest of my family are pretty well, Mother and Father thriving.

As you recount in one of the letters, it must have been painful for you, dear Anna, to get a screed meant for some piece he'd been trying to satisfy in London. It was generous of you to forgive him and I'm sure he has thanked you and would again, but for his death.

I am writing this to the address you gave in Liverpool, but I wonder if you are still there. Perhaps you moved on when you saw the reports of Denn's death in various newspapers and on TV, the Portakabins being visual. Politically, I expect you notice many changes here after a long absence abroad. I can assure you that Denn did worry about that business with the other girl so long ago. I never personally discovered what happened there, but I feel it would please you to know that he had enough sensitivity and conscience to regret it, whatever it was. His funeral had its dignified moments here and there in its little way, and I'm sure he would have been reasonably thrilled by it. Obviously, you could not be expected to attend, nor the floozy from London.

I imagine Denn would have been reluctant to give you his brother Tim's address, Denn wishing to have the sole run of your person if you returned, particularly in view of that grim business in the past. However, I do not have to be so unhelpful. The address is Cotreels, Several Avenue, Sligh, Angus, Scotland. Tim and his burgeoning family will, I'm sure, be delighted to see you and chew over old times. It might be a good notion to get to Scotland if the police are looking for you. There are plenty of mountain hiding spots, and what are known as glens.

Should you wish to call at Carthage, despite everything, I would, of course, be delighted to see you. When the hue and cry has died down a bit, it might even be possible for you to stay here a night or two, Anna. I would dearly like to introduce you to a former friend of mine, Mrs AV Ward, OBE, who has a great deal to be said for her, despite lumpiness, and who was entertaining Denn at least twice a week, mostly in her own lovely home, Fairholm. Her husband wants to kick her out of it now, apparently believing that *she* killed Dennis when spurned. Some might think a husband would be pleased if his wife killed a man who'd been banging her outside the marital fidelities, but this husband is very 'law and order'.

Well, Anna, were Dennis only here with me, I'm sure he would wish to pass on all the very best for the future, with the hope that you will iron out all your little probs, here and overseas.

Affectionate regards,
Jill

128

Carthage

Dear Tim,

A note to say thank you so much for making that long journey to Dennis's funeral and for the lovely flowers. Well, bleak Mr Winter seems to be really on the way now and the birds have left for sunnier climes – at least the sensible ones have! Not that our winters are usually all that bad. My own view is that we are extremely fortunate to live in such a temperate climate, and I have little sympathy with those who are always complaining about our weather.

Police have been here a lot, obviously, questioning, hinting. I'll have a word on the phone with you, Tim, about some of the things they said. It's not the kind of thing for a formal letter of acknowledgement, but important, maybe. They seem to have quite precise lines of inquiry, one of which would interest you, I think, and we'll talk about that, too, when I phone.

My very best to you and Sonia,
love,
Jill

129

Carthage
Tabbett Drive
Exall DL2 4NG

My dear Marie (if I may),
I'm so delighted to be able on his behalf to answer the letters you sent my husband not all that long ago, and which I've come across recently. I'm sure Dennis would have been honoured to reply in person, had he but lived. I note from your letter that you had been on a glorious tennis holiday in Italy previously to your letter, and this might well mean you failed to see in the national press that Dennis was killed in most unfortunate circumstances while Paul-Prying according to his little way. Tennis is a sport I've always promised myself participation in, yet never actually got around to. I trust you had plenty of conducive weather and, really, we did not do at all badly ourselves as to sunshine right into autumn, and especially late Sept. But now, change. This part of the year

is one of the most trying, I feel – the short days and diabolical winds – but we should not complain, should we, not when we recall what happened in New Orleans. I did hear the police wanted to talk to you, or to bravos possibly hired by you, about Dennis's death, but the tennis should be a total alibi, unless you left word for the bravos to act while you were away, the kind of move they, the police, would be used to, in their suspicious way, Marie.

As you recount it, it must have been deeply distressing for you, dear Marie, to get a letter meant for some ancient baggage he used to indulge, and I do not like to think of this really catastrophic item lying in that brilliantly modern London sorting office, so full of hurt and insult. It was generous of you to write and forgive him, and I'm sure Dennis would have eternally appreciated this fine gesture but for his death.

The Alain Delon research which you mention has reached its end, plainly, so that, much as you would have liked to see him on a further London visit, this is impossible. I parcelled up many of his research papers and tapes and offered them to a celebrated film archive in, as a matter of fact, London, who sent it back fast saying it was all crap. This probably will not surprise you any more than it did me, knowing Dennis.

Well, Marie, were Dennis only here with me, I'm sure he would wish to pass on all the very best for the future. Should you wish to claim the Alain Delon material as a memento of the very educational and aesthetic times you two must have had together, I can recover it from the black plastic refuse sacks before they are collected next Monday. Perhaps you could telephone. It's a treat to be able to take calls here now, certain that they are in that old James Bond phrase: 'For My Ears Only' – or eyes, actually, in the Bond books.

Yours affectionately,
Jill Seagrave

130

Memo:
Date: 2 December 2005
From: Bill Lestrange (counsellor)
To: Anne Pitt (supervisor)

At our next tutorial I would like to discuss the cases of DS and JS, a married couple whom I counselled for one session last week. They attended together and have said they will return. I believe they present a unique problem.

Some time ago they concluded that their marriage was beginning to deteriorate, both as a day-by-day partnership and sexually. They therefore decided that they would create fantasy lives for themselves and for each other in order, as JS puts it: 'to banish the humdrum, escape the confines of our established personalities, and restore excitement and edge to the relationship.' (Both are fairly articulate in different fashions.) To this end, they wrote letters to imaginary recipients about imaginary situations and imaginary people. When I say imaginary recipients, I mean that some were, in fact, made up, but others, such as the woman's mother and the man's brother may conceivably be real people (I have no present verified evidence either way), but no actual correspondence with them took place: the letters were concocted by JS and DS solely for each other. The pair also wrote letters from some of the 'correspondents', and occasionally a supposed woman neighbour and J's mother wrote to each other. In addition, they have one of their figment characters consulting a supposed counsellor, possibly akin to this one!

Many of the letters deal with supposed free-range sexual

adventures for both DS (husband) and JS (wife.) Some letters also hint at sexual partner-swapping parties held in their house. At the same time, a good number of the letters suggest that each spouse was in some sort of unspecified physical danger from the other, more particularly JS from DS. At one stage, JS's letters cease and she is described in DS's supposed letters to her parents as incapacitated by flu. At this point, a lover of JS, scared by developments, tries to get through by telephone to say he's off to live in Africa. She becomes enraged at being left to carry out a plan against DS herself.

It's possible JS and DS toyed with the notion of killing her (the fantasy JS) off by supposed flu, but she does reappear, though having suffered a beating with a tyre lever. You'll see I refer to hints and to unspecified factors. There is a general tone of vagueness and a shortage of crucial detail throughout much of the correspondence, extensive specimens of which they brought to the first consultation and which I have subsequently studied. There are hints that DS and his brother have been involved in some kind of serious violence, though this is left undefined. The house in their narrative is apparently full of elaborate telephonic recording and even bugging gadgets, making privacy difficult; but no reason is given, except, possibly DS's supposed nosiness and suspiciousness. It is these devices which J refers to as reasons for having to write ordinary, mailed letters in an electronic age. Occasionally, the unlikelihood of such very long letters, and on very sensitive matters, is recognized, as when J asks her friend C to destroy the one describing D's murder of a tramp in detail, liable to convict him if the killing were real. Also, one finds a deliberate contradictoriness, no doubt in an attempt to mirror the ambiguities of actual life. The accounts of DS's character, for instance, vary according to whether a letter is written by himself, by JS, or an imagined neighbour, Mrs AVW, with an unwise crush on DS, though her estimate of him varies.

Likewise, there are different explanations for postponement of a visit by JS's parents. To increase confusion, JS is sometimes branded as too imaginative in letters from her mother, and it is implied that perhaps the threats from her husband and some of the incidents are only in her head. I'm afraid I find this dizzying: we have the supposed letter from the mother suggesting all J's fears could be imaginary, which they are, but so is the letter from the mother imaginary, in which the question is raised. There is sometimes a send-up element present. For instance, the supposed transcript of the interview between J and a counsellor appears to parody sexual 'false memory syndrome' investigations.

A contrived shiftiness and imprecision in the letters was, they say, vital to their self-liberating purpose since it permitted each to fantasize in her/his own way, yet within the jointly accepted framework. Here and there, however, the letters do become very precise, for instance, in the reports of a fictitious private detective, N, engaged by the husband to monitor his wife's love-making in a Volvo. (N subsequently attempts blackmail in their narrative.) Hints about activities at the parties are often crude and physical – but occasionally euphemized. Some of the letters to JS's 'mother' become frank and/or suggestive and language can be coarse. There is a very long, detailed description of the imagined slaughter of the vagrant where some attempt at a literary style is attempted. They say they composed this and some other sections jointly.

Both JS and DS claim that their protracted programme of fantasizing brought enormous gains to their marriage, particularly sexually. 'We were able to see each other as if new people: adventurous, ungovernable, demanding, sought-after,' DS said. 'By seeming to swap partners we were also able to transform our own limited selves into personalities with more vitality and power: this is where the true "swap" took place, of course.' J says that the thrill of creativity reached into the rest of their lives, 'especially our bed lives', and that the posited threat from the other spouse made their actual love-making more comforting and meaningful, like continual reconciliations after fights. This improvement of their lives through fantasized promiscuity and violence now and then figures strongly in the fiction of their letters: e.g. JS says they made

208

ferocious love after the supposed murder by DS, comparing this with something she had seen in a film. Several sequences are deliberately devised to produce jealous excitement, as when D's brother tried to get in touch with a girl fancied by D.

JS and DS insult each other unsparingly – again to improve the reconciliation pleasures. They also seem to mock what they are doing in these letters by repeating whole chunks of parts of the correspondence (especially to DS's supposed lovers and his brother) word for word, except for changed names; like junk mail produced by computer. At times, they did work, in fact, on a word processor. Now and then they seem liable to bring the whole edifice of fantasy down by referring to high-flown fiction which has been written in letter form, especially a novel (TV adapted) called *Clarissa*. J says in one letter to her mother that she's glad their correspondence can't be put into a book because she destroys many of the letters. Likewise, of course, the scepticism of the mother about J's tales and the counsellor's reservations almost tear at the fabric of pretence.

Nevertheless, JS appears keen to give the letters a 'true' feel by referring at boring length to the weather and international politics, and by reverting suddenly to formula politeness: she will break off from denouncing D and say how much he would love to be remembered to them. It's like diplomats who spit at each other in private meetings but smile and shake hands at the press conference. In the middle of shockingly revelatory material she suddenly maunders on about the summer or Iraq. And she tries to create some kind of solid characterization for the J who writes the letters by giving her a rather exhibitionist style (! and italics), plus repeated cliché phrases – long suit, for instance. Also there are hints that J's childhood may hide unpleasant, formative secrets, and these add depth to the J persona.

Both J and D claim that this mixture of methods made the 'fantasy scenario', as they call it, workable and exciting. They felt the need to do something to counter the dull peacefulness of where they live, including the imagined weekend swingers' orgies. In this respect, they seem to represent a common paradox: they see and prize the social cachet of their property in suburbia, but disdain those qualities that produce the social cachet. Some other parts of the writing, besides the description of the tramp's murder, may also have been done jointly, for instance, the private detective's reports. Such actual shared creativity also brought them closer, they claim.

But, although their play acting was successful for a long period, they came to find eventually that the 'milieu of artifice', as DS calls it, had its own built-in self-destructive element. On this account they decided to seek marriage guidance and came to Communicate. They were referred to me as their counsellor. As time passed, they discovered that, in order to maintain its success, the fantasy had to be continually cranked up to a greater intensity, and less credibility. JS, while seemingly conducting a settled affair with one man, G, begins another very risky liaison with the vagrant P, much of it based on avid groping in the reading room of the public library!

As the law of diminishing returns increasingly took over, they seemed to find themselves ultimately pushed into the kind of situation they played with via the flu letters: that is, the violent death of one of the principals. Now, though, it was DS who had to be fictionally killed; and apparently by JS. She planned to act in concert with her lover G, using a waste land site with Portakabins which she had discovered with P the vagrant! G supplies the gun, obtained from former student friends who'd belonged with G to a firearms club. But G has run abroad to avoid involvement, leaving J to carry out the execution solo. (Earlier hints suggested D could be seen off through an arranged stepladder accident.) Several people are suspected of D's killing, but JS remains more or less in the clear.

The problem now, of course, is that their stimulating fantasy experiences are no longer available. It was essential that each should be able to titillate the other with supposed extra marital behaviour, titillate and sometimes shock. The poor way G absconds might be seen as a comment on men generally, including DS. Clearly, it is not logical for the 'dead' DS to continue to figure through his own letters or those of others, except as a funeral topic. I gather that the wife continued with some cruel letters to a couple of DS's supposed 'other' women after his 'demise'. But these tail-end letters of the fantasy have not contributed to the health of the marriage and they feel themselves once more to be sinking; possibly even faster than before, because the loss of their constructed world has hit them so severely.

They know, of course, that they could begin an entirely new fantasy situation for themselves whenever they wish, but are perceptive enough to realize that, in time, the satisfactions of fantasy are likely once again to dwindle and disappear. It is about the wisdom or not of creating further fictional lives for themselves that they wish to talk to me as their counsellor. In turn, I would like to discuss this with you, since I do not feel well-qualified to help them, their difficulties being outside the range of my experience and training. DS has come across a quotation by, I believe, Mark Twain, which he says goes something like this: 'Do not part with your illusions. When they are gone you may still exist, but you have ceased to live.' Both of them are half inclined to believe this, but only half; experience seems to tell them something different. My admittedly tentative reading of their case leads me to think that, if they abandon fantasy, they will move into actual, competitive promiscuity, and from there possibly into violence. The obvious reference is the Frederick and Rosemary West case. I shall be grateful for your views.

BL
2 December 2005

131

*W*ell, an advance – and such an advance! I'm actually invited into the Seagrave home, Carthage, and Jill and I talk – and such talk! We bump into each other at the super-market and she says, as if it's entirely usual, that we should have a coffee together at her place, and, 'Why not today, Kate?' I'm amazed, but try not to show it. And, of course, I agree. That strange remoteness Vince and I have noticed in her lately seems entirely gone. Something has happened to her, that's clear. Yes, it's clear, clear, clear, that something has happened to her, but what it is that's happened is not clear at all. Lately, I seem to have become liable to these vague impressions of big changes in people's minds and outlooks. It's the same sort of powerful, though entirely undefined feeling, I've had about Vince himself. Even during the first few words of greeting spoken between Jill and me near the Homecare shelves at Tesco's, I'm aware of a shift in her personality. And then the invitation back to Carthage and what we eventually talk about there mightily confirms this earlier reaction. Or, really, it's not what we talk about, but what she talks about. I listen gobsmacked and throw in the occasional, very occasional, word!

We are in a pleasantly furnished rear room, looking out upon the garden. Part of the cormorant's tail is visible to the right. The floor is varnished hardwood boards, with one central red and black patterned Persian rug. There are two Edwardian style armchairs under dark-blue loose covers and a blue leather chesterfield sofa, also Edwardian in style. A fine, mahogany chiffonier stands against one wall. The fireplace is narrow and surrounded by tiles decorated with wild flower motifs, the *tiles possibly reclaimed from some demolished property, again perhaps Edwardian or even Victorian. On a polished Pembroke table, near French doors to the garden, is a heavy, old-style, circular-dial, grubby, cream-coloured telephone. We sit in armchairs facing each other, nursing our coffee mugs. Small side tables would seem genteel and naff in this room. We both have a real china plate containing a couple of biscuits propped on one fat arm of our chairs. Dennis is not at home.*

At first, the chat is generalities about the neighbourhood, the shops and stores, the topiary and television. I express my deep approval of the room and how it's furnished. I express special admiration for the boarded floor and single, beautiful rug, saying I so much prefer that kind of layout to fitted carpet. She nods in acknowledgement and then starts to giggle. I'm naturally perplexed, wait for her to explain why my remark – quite sincerely meant – is amusing. She goes silent momentarily, as if wondering whether she should *and* will *explain. So I stay silent, too.*

And then comes the real revelation, though only gradually. At first, I'm still baffled. Well, it is *cryptic. She tells me that when she looks at the boarded floor and the rug she can often see something utterly different. 'Oh?' I reply, surprised. Wouldn't* anyone *be surprised?*

What she sees, she answers, is, in fact, some of that hated wall-to-wall carpeting, 'Beigish mostly.' That was the phrase, 'beigish mostly.' It sticks because it would seem so utterly wrong for this room, 'beigish mostly', fitted carpet – dull and serviceable. I reply that I don't understand. And she comments, no, she didn't actually expect me to. She adds that when she said just now that what she sees 'in fact' was the 'beigish mostly' fitted carpet she didn't really mean 'in fact', but its total opposite – i.e. it's what she sometimes *imagines.*

I comment that everybody lives a little in their imagination, but usually they imagine something they'd like better than the real, such as imagining one had landed a couple of million on the lottery, instead of the ten pounds one actually has *landed. I say 'beigish mostly' carpet doesn't seem to me better than what she has, but definitely inferior. Again she nods and again stays quiet for a while. Then the explanations start to flow. She says that she and Dennis had come to feel so flattened and depressed by the sedateness of their lives in Tabbett Drive – this was her word, 'sedateness' – so crushed by this sedateness that they'd decided to create another setting for themselves and do it mainly through letter writing on the word processor and occasional supposed commentaries by marriage guidance experts and so on. She says she found my remark about the bare boards and single rug amusing because in one or more of her supposed letters she would refer to the fitted carpeting all through the house – 'beigish mostly'– which made it easy for Dennis to approach her silently and perhaps surprise her doing something she didn't want him to know about, such as writing a frank letter! And this, she says, typifies one of the main points about the correspondence from Jill and from Dennis: each of them feels a terrible fear of the other and describes this in their letters to relatives and friends. Jill apparently mentions in some of her letters a highly sophisticated, up-to-the-minute telephone and recording system at Carthage, which helped oppress and frighten her – instead of the actual ancient looking receiver. Their imagined lives took in sexual unfaithfulness, snooping by a private detective, orgies behind closed curtains, disgraceful behaviour in a public library reading room, and, eventually two murders, one of Dennis himself by Jill.*

I'm in shock, of course, listening to all this. It's true I had suspicions not long ago that she and Dennis might be into some kind of mind's eye, trance-like world now and then, but I would never have realized the extent of this. Perhaps I look disbelieving. She puts her mug down on the floor, goes to the chiffonier and opens a cupboard. It is stuffed with papers. She takes a random handful and brings it to me. I see the sheets are, indeed, typed letters and what seem to be detective reports of surveillance of sexual encounters in a car. I put my own coffee mug down and glance quickly through the material. I spot a phrase saying that in the weekend parties she has learned to accept that anything can be regarded as normal as long as all parties agree. On another page she calls Dennis a venomous swine for buying her a totally unsuitable caftan as a birthday present, specifically because he knows it will make her look frightful. In a letter to one of his girlfriends, Dennis speaks of possibly bringing the marriage to an end.

There's plenty more, but I don't need it. I believe her now. I ask whether all this fantasy worked. She says it did, but that it's become more or less played out. They have taken it to the limit, and both now feel an appalling deprivation. It is so bad that they have begun to get real *marriage counselling – not the sort they imagined for their figments. This troubles me. I comprehend what it is that has altered her. And I fear that if they have become so catastrophically restless in the Drive again, they will move away. I still need them here, regardless of the weird stratagems they employed to make it tolerable. I ask straight out whether she thinks they might have to look for somewhere else to live. She takes back the papers she gave me and shuts them in the cupboard. She returns to her chair, picks up the mug of coffee and begins to talk vigorously about the weather and Iraq.*

132

Carthage
Tabbett Drive
6 December 2005

My dear Mother,

Well, here we are, approaching Christmas post haste and one can feel a real sharpness in the air. Mum, I am rather embarrassed by what I'm going to tell you now – which is why I'm putting it in a letter, rather than talking about it in one of our many phone calls.

You see, Mother, Dennis and I have been playing a wonderful make-believe game to keep ourselves amused and lively, and this entailed writing letters here, there and everywhere, and receiving them, too. We wrote the lot, of course – those we, as it were, sent, and those we, as it were, received. You, naturally, were one of the chief people I 'wrote to'. We had to communicate by letter because this house was supposedly crammed with electronic snooping equipment! Oh, yes, you 'received' a whole sackful of sometimes quite raunchy mail, and I have to tell you that your replies grew very anxious now and then. Do you remember, Ma? No, I thought not! All make-believe.

I'm not sure whether to go for goose or turkey this Christmas. I do love turkey in all its forms, but it seems so unadventurous to buy it year after year and give no other fowl a chance – a chance to be devoured, that is! The thing is, our 'script' – Denn's and mine – had to come to an end ultimately, of course, and we both felt very down when that happened. In fact, we became so depressed that we have begun seeing a marriage guidance counsellor in the Communicate organization. It's pretty clear he hasn't a clue on how to deal with our problem.

As for Yule gifts, you must let us know in good time (and on the quiet, of course) what Father would like. I will take personal responsibility for choosing something exactly right for you, knowing your fine taste.

The betting is once again against a white Christmas, I hear. I can't say I'm sorry since the birds have terrible trouble feeding in those conditions, and drinking, especially.

Your loving daughter,
Jill

133

My dear Tim,

It seems an age since we've been in touch, and yet, in a sense, it is not at all – though you would not be aware of that, I fear!

The point is, Jill and I have been playing an elaborate game of fantasizing for quite a while, the essence of which was that we devised imaginary letters to and from various folk, some real – like your good self – and some made up. I can tell you, Tim, you have received some quite forceful and even sinister letters from me, and I, in my turn, have received some quite lecherous ones from you!

But the pastime played itself out at last, of course, as it was bound to. It finished, as a matter of fact – well not quite of *fact*, but you know what I mean! – with your dear brother's death, shot by Jill, following the murder of one of her lovers by me and threats to another. All action, you see! I can tell you, we both miss our excursions into sexy, violent dreaming. Indeed, we felt so bereft that we decided to see a marriage guidance counsellor and discuss our plight. Frankly, I don't think he has ever met such a situation before and seems in a dither about whether to recommend another period of fantasy or some different solution.

Have you any ideas, Tim?

Your loving brother,
Dennis

134

God, did I call that a revelation when Jill Seagrave invited me back to her house – so fucking chummy and imperative all of a fucking sudden, the deceitful, lascivious bitch – 'Why not today, Kate?' So, I agree and she goes into that fascinating, hot, brilliantly irrelevant spiel about her fantasy life. The real revelation came later, didn't it, and without the least bit of fantasy involved. Real, real, real and sickening. Her performance that day was presumably meant as some kind of distraction. A cover-up. And, because of my damn stupidity and dim willingness to believe her, it worked. I was supposed to think, here's a woman whose main life is in the mind and the imagination, whose pleasure is dreams and who yearns now for more of them to satisfy her. Oh, yeah? No wonder I had difficulty understanding her properly. And no wonder I felt puzzled by an indefinable change in Vincent, my dear husband. Well, I mustn't kick a corpse – 'Don't speak ill of the dead', and all that. In fact, I don't feel much like speaking about any of it. Let's use one of the local press cuttings to tell the foul, disgustingly true and, yes, real, real, real tale, shall we?

CRIME OF PASSION
Prosperous Exall husband guilty of murder

A highly successful insurance broker was sent to prison for life yesterday following his conviction for the murder of his wife's lover, a close neighbour in one of the most select suburbs of Exall. The judge rejected a plea from defence lawyers for a lighter sentence. They argued that the killing was partly justified as a crime passionnel, the broker having surprised his wife and her lover in bed at Carthage, their executive style, spacious home.

But the judge ruled that British law did not recognize the category crime passionnel and sentenced thirty-seven-year-old Dennis Seagrave to life imprisonment for the murder of Vincent Callis, aged thirty-five, who was killed with a hedge-clipping tool in the detached, prestige property of the Seagraves in tree-lined Tabbett Drive. Callis and his thirty-three-year-old wife Katherine (Kate) had only recently come to live in the Drive, but soon built a friendship with the Seagraves who had been established there for more than four years.

The court heard that out of this neighbourly friendship a secret love relationship recently developed between Vincent Callis and Jill Seagrave. Returning unexpectedly from a visit to a client in February, Dennis Seagrave was appalled to hear giveaway, unmistakable sounds from upstairs and deliberately selected a machete-style blade from the many hedge-cutting tools in the utility room, then went to the bedroom and fatally attacked Vincent Callis with it, inflicting twenty-seven wounds. Dennis Seagrave practised topiary as a hobby – the art of creating animal figures – in the high, thick Carthage hedges. Among animals and birds he has depicted there were a bison, a cormorant and a peacock. The utility room contained many of his topiary instruments.

His wife Jill escaped injury and gave evidence of what happened on that futile February afternoon. Police said that Dennis Seagrave had removed his shoes before mounting the stairs to the bedroom because Carthage had no wall-to-wall carpets, only varnished floorboards and rugs, and his footsteps might otherwise have been heard on the landing. The prosecution claimed that the careful choice of the machete-style blade and Seagrave's similarly careful removal of his shoes indicated a calculated intent to make the attack. The jury clearly accepted this. (Carthage was a prominent city in classical times, important in the Punic Wars.)

Detective Superintendent Trevor Mintrom, who lead the investigation, told the court that when police did a routine search of Carthage following discovery of the murder they found papers in a downstairs cupboard which seemed to show that Dennis and Jill Seagrave had for many months conducted, via imaginary correspondence and fictitious accounts of inter-views and reports from counsellors, a highly-charged fantasy life based on promiscuous adultery. Psychiatrist Amanda Lowell of the famed London Staleyworth Institute, called by the prosecution as an expert witness, told the court that such fantasizing was not uncommon among materially successful couples approaching middle age. She explained that their very success seemed to make them question sceptically what pleasure they had actually gained from these achievements. They could slip into intolerable boredom, and seek comfort through 'elaborately' constructed personal fables.'

Dr Lowell said, 'The removal or collapse of such fables – such alternative experience – can bring about a severe undermining of morale, leading even to despair and possible compensatory extreme behaviour.' The prosecution argued that Mrs Seagrave had suffered such a breakdown of morale and in her search for compensatory excitement and affection had turned to her neighbour, Vincent Callis.

Dr Lowell also said in evidence that although someone taking part in a fantasy life might be able to tolerate the supposed ill behaviour of others as part of that fantasy, this did not in any way make such behaviour in another or others acceptable as real experience. In fact, it might lead to a more vigorous reaction against such behaviour when met with in actuality because of a dread – possibly a subconscious dread – that the unreal was taking over. In other words, Dr Lowell said, a fear of the onset of madness. The prosecution alleged this process – the fierce need to assert the real demands of faithfulness in marriage – was what drove Dennis Seagrave to murder, when he discovered his wife's disloyalty.

Mrs Seagrave did not attend court to hear her husband sentenced. She was believed to be staying with relatives or friends. She did not answer the telephone yesterday nor respond to callers at Carthage. Neighbours in Tabbett Drive said the house appeared unoccupied for the past few days. 'This kind of tragic event is not at all what we are used to in Tabbett Drive,' said one neighbour, who did not wish to be named.